About the Author

In 2011, after many years of dedicated study in the field of Personal Development and other related topics, I set up Mind and Achievement Ltd to help people from all walks of life to achieve their dreams and goals. Through my books, videos and seminars, I encourage people to set their minds for achievement.

www.tonybrassington.com

Disclaimer

Please note that this book is a work of fiction, and as such all characters, business names, clubs or associations, and events are all fictitious, and have no known connection with anyone, past or present.

To all those who wish to succeed in life,

I wish you every success.

Tony Brassington

Introduction to

The Well-Travelled Book Series

You may be the first reader of this book, which is part of The Well-Travelled Book Series, or one of its many subsequent readers, but in either case, you are now holding in your hands a very special and unique book. The Well-Travelled Book Series is the first series of its kind to be shared and distributed in this way, and this book will be certain to have many imitators in the future, but this series of books is the original trailblazer that led the way.

There is a very memorable line in the Johnny Depp film, *The Ninth Gate,* when two antique book dealers, who are identical twins, are discussing a very rare and valuable book.

"All books have a destiny of their own, even a life of their own."

This quote encourages you to think about the life of a book. The saddest thing of all for a book must be to gather dust on a shelf, never to be read, looked at, or even moved occasionally, year after year, decade after decade. There is even a Japanese word for this, *Tsundoku*, which defines the habit of buying books and never reading them and then storing them with other unread books.

"There is something sad about an unread book."
Thomas Hardy – *Tess of the D'Urbervilles*

The author of any book wants to believe that the time and great effort he or she put into creating their work leads to a book which is being well read in the wider world. Whilst it is true that too many books sit on shelves gathering dust, some books are indeed very well-travelled. Some books have the power to lead the reader to great life-changing discoveries and personal insights, and I would even go as far as to say that some books have a special energy of their own - the best books have a combination of all three. I would like to think that this is a book with those three qualities.

My intended purpose for this book is firstly, and just for fun, to demonstrate over time just how far and wide a book can travel around the world, secondly, to spread greater awareness and understanding of the Universal Laws, and, finally, to promote giving and sharing every time this book is passed along.

In order for this book to promote sharing, please give it away after reading it.   Give it to a friend or colleague, or give it to a total stranger. For example, if you are on holiday, give it to another holidaymaker after you have read it. You may read and share it on a coach, bus or train, in the park, in a coffee shop, or anywhere you can think of. This can add greatly to the life and adventures of this Well-Travelled Book, while also allowing you the opportunity to give something to others.

After reading this book, please sign and date it, and then share this book with another person.

Contents

A few words from the Author

The Many Lovers

of

Henry Farmer

A few words from the Author

I conceived the idea for this story while I was writing the first two books in *The Well-Travelled Book Series,* and the time has now come to write it. Originally, I envisaged this story as a farce, a comedy, a great exaggeration, but I can now see that it contains so much more than that.

From the title of the book, you can easily guess a certain amount of the book's content. I was uneasy about the main theme of the content, to begin with, and had to ask myself two questions before writing it, *why I wanted to write it?* And, *what can the reader gain from reading it?*

I needed to understand why I wanted to write this story because I have seen too many stories written by men which are simply an outlet for the dark corners of their minds, a Freudian-slip of sorts set in print; if that was all it was, then, for me there would be no point in writing it.

I believe this story addresses a great many topics that are of interest and importance to virtually all of us. For example, why do some people appear to be blessed with good luck in many areas of life? More than that, in my own life I have witnessed a rare number of people succeeding, where others would expect to meet with failure. When you think about it, we have all seen someone fly in the face of the best-accepted success wisdom and appear to be doing okay on the surface of things, but are they really? Surely we all must ultimately follow the same *Laws of the*

Universe, and *The Laws of Success,* yet on the surface of it some people and businesses appear not to?

To answer my second question, *what can the reader gain from reading it?* Just like every other title in *The Well-Travelled Book Series,* first, there is a strong story plot and many interesting and diverse characters to help the story to unfold and reveal its message. Yet, this is not a book that shouts its unveiled wisdom out loud, but the discerning reader will discover many layers and truths hidden within the story. In many ways, this is a book of my observations. In my own life, I have seen many people and businesses that think the rules of the game do not apply to them, or those that think they can ignore them without any cost or peril. Therefore, this story is not quite as much of an exaggeration as it first might appear.

In my opinion, this book meets the same criteria as the other titles in *The Well-Travelled Book Series.*

Also, I have endeavoured to write this story so that it can be equally enjoyed by both sexes.

Tony Brassington

Stones

Chapter 1

"Now stand still Carla while I pin this badge on you," Lynn said as she tried to attach a badge on to Carla's t-shirt with the word PRESS written boldly across it, as they both stood in the Moonraker Hotel's car park in the city of Bath.

"Honestly Lynn, you reporters are so bossy," Carla jokingly replied.

"There you are now, with that badge now in place you could almost pass for a member of the press; well almost," she said with dry sarcasm.

"What do you mean, well almost?"

"You just look too sweet and innocent Carla."

Lynn shook her head in mock disbelief.

"Honestly Carla, I have tried so hard over the past two years to bring you down to my level; a few years back I thought we were making some progress too, but now look at you."

"Well, that is me." Carla pondered, "Well, do you have any tips for me today, about being a reporter, I mean, if anyone asks, what do I say, or how do I have to act?"

"Oh my dear girl, haven't you been paying attention to me since we met?" Lynn said in mocking humour. "Well, here we are both 34 years old and yet it appears that I still have so much left to teach you."

Carla looked bemused, "Okay, so go on then, please teach me a little something. For example, if I have to ask a question like a reporter would…"

"Oh, that is so easy Carla, my dear girl. Just ask blunt rude insensitive questions, and then ask another before they are halfway through answering the first, then you should get away with it. Got it?"

Carla sighed a little in good humour, "Anyway, just remind me again why you talked me into coming here with you today?"

Lynn peered at Carla intently, paused and then said, "Well, firstly Carla my dear girl, despite all your shortcomings, I remain your best friend, possibly your only friend, and there is no one else here on earth that you would rather spend the day with today."

"Oh, is that right? Thanks for reminding me."

"It's no problem… Now you see that tall old guy over there. His name is Wilson, and he is the real reason we are here."
They both turned towards the hotel's main entrance, where a group of reporters stood around talking.

"Lynn, which guy? There is a large group of reporters over there."

"Don't go into investigative journalism dear, you'll never make it. I said the tall old guy." Lynn sighed and then impatiently said, "The tallest one dear."

"You don't need to be rude, Lynn. I see him now…"
Lynn butted in, "Yes, well that is him. The guy with no distinguishing features. Just look at him. Nothing about him is attractive, his face is, well, it is just simply grey and featureless, his hair… oh well enough said about his hair. And he dresses like he

2

buys all his clothes from a charity shop and has slept in them for days."

"Don't you mean nights?" Carla giggled.

Lynn smirked, "Days, nights, whatever. He looks like he has slept in them, and he probably has." Then her voice turned to one of respect and admiration. "Let me tell you something about Wilson. No one can sniff out a fresh, great new story like he can. You might be surprised how many reporters in that group over there actually follow Wilson around wherever he goes, because they know how good he is. None of them will admit it though." Lynn chuckled. "Three of them got caught out a few years back, when Wilson took an unexpected holiday and they followed him all the way to the beach thinking that he was following some big story. The bloody fools!"

"Well, I agree he doesn't look much."

"No, he doesn't look much fun at all, but I'd have his love child if he dropped a big enough story in my lap."

A satisfied smile appeared on Lynn's face.

Carla noticed this and asked, "You are joking, right, surely."

"Oh yes, of course, darling," although her eyes did not appear to deny it as much as she did.

"Anyway, that is why we are here. From time to time, he gives a few reporters like me, the guys he respects, a few scraps of new story leads, and this is one of them. If you take a closer look at that crowd of reporters over there you will notice that there are some pretty big names from the field of journalism amongst them. And if it wasn't for Wilson none of them would be here. Think about it. We are about to witness the opening of a refurbished hotel lobby. Just how newsworthy can that be? The Mayor of Bath is turning up to officially open it for them, but even so, so what! Something pretty special and very newsworthy is going to happen, or else why would Wilson and his followers, me included, be here?"

Carla thought about that for a moment, "I suppose that you must be right about that."

"Oh yes, I'm right, and I thought to myself why not share whatever it is that we are about to be treated to in there with my old mate Carla. It will make a good start to your holiday, before you go off painting flowers, or walking about farmers' fields in search of a tree to hug to find your inner-self, or whatever it is you are planning to do on your two weeks of holiday.

"Tree hugging indeed," she said dismissively before adding, "And there is nothing wrong with a bit of art. I used to be good at it back at school. I should have stuck with it. I am about to begin a two-week holiday in the country. I probably will not get around to any painting though, just me and my sketchbook, it will be good for me. Escape, draw and relax."

"I am pleased for you, Carla. I hope you have a great time. Truly, I do," Lynn said, faking a concerned tone of voice, followed by a playful wink, before adding, "I hope they have a potter's-wheel there for you too, my dear."

Carla shook her head a little and smiled at her friend's teasing. Then Lynn added, "Just promise me that you will not take up singing again, please my dear!" Carla frowned upon hearing that and looked a little hurt by it too.

Just then, the manager of the Moonraker Hotel came out through the main entrance and invited the assembled press to come inside. He directed everyone to an area in the hotel's main lobby, set aside for the press and then addressed them.

"Okay then, good morning everyone. First, let me thank you all for coming. This is going to be a very special opening today, one that I am sure you will never forget. Over the next twenty minutes or so, a number of specially invited guests will be arriving. The Mayor of Bath is already here, he is sitting in my office as we speak. So, it won't be too long now."

Carla looked around the lobby. The area that the Mayor was due to open was surrounded by a tall, black, crushed velvet curtain, which was centrally placed in the lobby. As the hotel manager walked back to his office, Carla couldn't help but overhear what some other members of the press were saying.

She looked at Lynn and noticed how her eyes appeared to say, "keep quiet."

Carla looked down and spotted a small red light in Lynn's hand meaning that her Dictaphone was now recording. Carla made eye contact with Lynn, and Lynn gave a friendly wink back. Carla remembered hearing Lynn say so many times before, "You have to know when to talk, and you have to know when to shut up and listen."

Clearly, it was a time to listen, or at least Lynn thought it was. Carla heard a female reporter somewhere behind her quietly talking to a colleague.

"Well, I have heard a rumour that it has something to do with stones, boulders, rocks, or something like that."
Another voice to the side of them said, "You will laugh at a rumour I heard about this opening ceremony today."
The female voice replied, "Go on Terry, spill, what you have heard."

"No, really I shouldn't because it must be total rubbish."
"Terry," she said insistently.

"Okay, well if you insist, but don't shoot the messenger. Well, here it is. Do you remember Nikola Tesla? 1856 to 1943? I'm good with people and dates."

"No, I can't say that I have heard of him."

"Well, Nikola Tesla was the real genius that helped to create the world that we now live in. It was him who came up with things like, alternating current, the fluorescent light bulb, lasers and so much more."

Another voice joined in, "Yes, I've heard of him. He was very flamboyant and charismatic too, a real showman. Some of the old photographs of him show him holding a lit light bulb in his hand, but with no wires, and other photographs show him surrounded by a shower of electrical sparks. What a genius."

Terry continued, "Well, I heard that Nikola Tesla has been working on this project for months, behind wooden screens, but he could not have, because as I said he died in 1943."

The conversations continued as Lynn and Carla listened with interest to many of the reporters enthusiastically talking about the life and work of Nikola Tesla. As the minutes quickly went by the hotel lobby filled with guests. The hotel manager and the Mayor took their places near the front. At the appointed time the hotel manager stood up and took a small silver receptionist bell from his pocket and began pressing the button on top of it to get everyone's attention.

"Good morning everyone, and thank you for coming along today. As many of you will know, there has been some building work going on in the centre of the hotel lobby behind these wooden screens for some months now. We have tried very hard to keep the work going on here behind those wooden screens a big secret for months. All that I have been allowed to say until

6

now is that this hotel is building a very special attraction, or exhibit if you prefer, for our hotel lobby. It is a world first. I am absolutely certain that there is nothing like it anywhere else in the world. But that is enough from me for now. As you will soon discover, seeing is believing. So, could I ask you all to give a big round of applause for the Mayor of Bath?"

The Mayor stood up as the applause began, and as he did so, he looked the hotel manager in the eye and smiled with intrigue; then he addressed the assembled crowd.

"I am looking forward to seeing what is lying behind this curtain. They haven't told me what it is either. I have to confess, that at first, I did take a bit of persuading to come to this event today since I was not certain what I was going to open, but I have been assured that it is something very special, not just for this hotel, but for the city of Bath also. So, I think that it is time we all found out what is behind this curtain."

The Mayor turned around to face the black curtain, and reached out his hand and grasped a thick golden rope with tassels at its ends. For a moment he looked a little apprehensive, and then he turned towards the crowd and said, "I now declare that this special exhibit in the Moonraker Hotel is open for the entire world to see."

With that, he gave the rope a gentle pull and the black curtains surrounding the exhibit came down. Carla noticed and thought it a little strange, that there appeared to be no framework of any kind to hold the curtains up, and when she looked to the floor where the curtains had fallen, there was now no sign of them. Had they vanished? Then she looked at the exhibit itself. Surrounding the exhibit was a number of chrome pillars about waist height with a thick red rope between each one.

7

Six large boulders lay on the floor, three of them were sarsen stones from somewhere in Wiltshire, and the other three were granite stones from Cornwall. The boulders were arranged alternately, one after another in an ill-defined circle. There was a moment of silence and then the crowd began to clap, but without any real enthusiasm and for a short duration.

The Mayor looked a little uncomfortable and cut the manager a questioning look. The manager then stood up and gestured to the Mayor to take his seat again, which he did immediately.

One of the reporters murmured sarcastically, "Is this it? We came all this way for rocks lying on the floor."

The room was virtually silent, as the hotel manager turned to face the crowd, slowly a knowing confident grin came across his face, which indicated that there was more to this than just six large stone boulders lying on the floor. Without saying another word the manger fully stretched out his right arm and turned gesturing to the back to the hotel lobby.

A man's footsteps could then be heard approaching, as he emerged from the shadows. He was tall and he was wearing an old fashioned, but well-cut suit. His hair was dark and wavy with a central parting, and he had a well-groomed moustache. He carried himself with elegance and confidence. He exuded natural charm. The manager sat back down in his seat, but now he had a beaming, proud, radiant smile on his face. The man walked to the centre of the stones, and then he smiled at the room full of silent people. He reached inside his jacket pocket and pulled out a light bulb. He placed the light bulb centrally in his other palm, where it illuminated. Some of the crowd were quite intrigued by this and some people clapped their hands in approval. He put the light bulb into the first hand and it went out again before he finally placed it back inside his jacket. Then he spoke aloud, in a good voice, slowly and confidently, "Please let me remind you all of something I once said."

He paused for a moment and then continued, "The present is theirs; the future, for which I really worked, is mine."

He paused to let those words sink in with the crowd and then he continued, "My name is Nikola Tesla. In the past, I offered this World, clean, free, renewable energy. I offered this World an electric car that could draw its required energy directly from the environment, for free, using my well-proven principles. I have come back to you now, only for a short while, to remind you of these things, and may these six stones sat around me here, be further evidence of the truth that I speak."

He stretched out both of his arms, with the palm of each hand facing the floor. He remained tranquil. There was a faint rumbling that sounded like distant thunder. The lights were dimmed, as small blue and purple coloured electrical sparks began to dance around the floor between the stones.

A succession of loud noises increased in intensity like the sound of thunder and lightning on a stormy night. When the noise and sparks reached their threshold, the dancing electrical sparks on the ground appeared to jump up higher and be drawn into Tesla's open palms. There was silence again, as Tesla knelt, placing both of his palms on one of the sarsen stones, after which it began to rise off the floor. He stood back up and looked at the floating stone which was now as high as his knee. Tesla moved back to the centre of the circle and appeared to be waiting.

After a few moments the other two sarsen stones, through some unseen connection with the first stone, began to also slowly rise off the floor also, until they reached the same height as the first sarsen stone.

He now stretched out his arms again and the loud rumbles of thunder returned, as before, accompanied by electrical sparks shooting up from the floor, to be received into Tesla's open palms again. Silence returned.

Tesla walked over to one of the granite stones still at rest on the floor, and he knelt before it and placed his hands upon it. Soon, that stone also began to rise to the same height as the other stones. Tesla returned to the centre of the circle again as the remaining two granite stones also began to float. He gave everyone one of his charismatic smiles and then he raised his arms above his head.

A new series of deafening crashes of thunder and lightning emanated from the floor. The noise was growing louder and louder and the electrical sparks were getting ever brighter and more intense with each passing moment. People began to feel uncomfortable and put their hands over their eyes to avoid the brightness. Carla tried to keep looking at Tesla for as long as she could, but he was now very hard to see amid the bright electrical sparks. All of a sudden, there was one final deafening roar of thunder, and a flash of lightning and a bright light filled the whole room. Silence followed, and when Carla looked again, Tesla was now nowhere to be seen. "The stones, the stones, look at them now!" Someone cried.

Carla then focused on the stones, which were now floating much higher than before, a child could easily walk under them, if it wasn't for the surrounding rope barrier to keep people at bay. But the stones did more than float. They slowly and randomly rotated and rolled over. None of them was static.

Someone began to clap, and then a few more people joined in until the whole room was united in enthusiastic applause. Then coloured strobe lighting units came on, one for each stone; which enhanced the effect of these floating, moving stones.

"Oh wow, Lynn. Would you look at that? I have never seen anything like it before."

Carla turned to look at Lynn, who was uncharacteristically speechless.

After the applause died down the hotel manager and the Mayor said a few parting words, but no one was listening to them. Everyone's attention was on the floating stones which were now illuminated in a variety of colours by the strobe lights.

An hour and a half later, many people and journalists were still hanging around. Lynn and Carla were back in the car park with other members of the press. Most of them were either on the phone or working away on a laptop spreading their news. Lynn now pressed the off button on her Dictaphone.

"Is it a wrap, then, Lynn?"

"Oh yes, it is a wrap."

She put her Dictaphone back in her handbag and pulled out a top-quality compact camera.

"In a while, I'll go back inside and take a few pictures of those floating stones, when there are fewer people about. It is worth a little wait in order to get some better pictures. Right now those stones are still surrounded by the world and his dog."

"Good idea. If you wait a bit you will get the incredible photographs you want."

Carla pondered for a moment, and then asked, "Do you always leave your Dictaphone recording for so long after the event?"

Lynn smiled, "Oh yes, the tricks of the trade, and if I had been writing away on a notepad I would have missed so much. By leaving my Dictaphone recording I have also caught my colleagues debating things like whether that was an actor we just saw in there, or Tesla himself?"

"But Lynn, how could it be Tesla himself. As one of the guys said earlier in there, Tesla died back in 1943?"

"Well, I caught it all on my Dictaphone. Many of my colleagues got their phones out and researched Tesla on the internet. They said the likeness of the man we saw today was amazingly close."

"Yes, but he is still dead isn't he, so it couldn't have been him?"

Lynn smiled, "Some of my colleagues were also talking about magnetic fields and time travel, or at least the theory behind it all, and a few minutes ago one guy said to Wilson, "If anyone knew about such things as magnetic fields and time travel, Tesla would have.""

Carla shrugged her shoulders, "Well, time travel is not for me. Sorry, I just cannot buy into that one."

"I admit, it is also a concept that I personally find very hard to grasp also. I will research it a bit more this evening before I write this story up."

Lynn paused and then added, "Actually, for me as a freelance reporter this story is a real one-off. Anyway, I will write it and offer it to my industry contacts to see who wants to buy it. One thing is for sure, if those stones remain floating around in that hotel lobby, the story isn't going to go away any time soon, even if some people find it hard to believe."

Just then Lynn received a text message. She took her phone out of her pocket and glanced at it, and smiled as she read the message, "You see Carla, I knew this day would work out well."

Lynn looked at a group of reporters with Wilson standing amongst them, and Wilson gave her an acknowledging nod. Then, Lynn turned back to Carla with a satisfied smile, "Wilson wants to talk to me before he leaves. I bet he has a new story for me, something good that he is too busy to cover himself."

Lynn became lost in her thoughts for a few seconds as her mind began to speculate about what kind of story Wilson might have for her, and Carla realised that it was now time for her to leave.

"I am pleased for you Lynn. And by the way, I have enjoyed myself today, I have. Whatever we just saw happen in there, it was memorable, to say the least."

Lynn gave a nod and tried to return her thoughts to the present moment. Then she gave a pleasant smile and said to Carla, uncharacteristically nicely, "I hope you have a great couple of week's holiday on that farm you are going to."

"Oh, I will." She quietly added, "Let me know later what kind of story Wilson wants you to cover."

Lynn's eyes said it all in reply. She looked so excited and eager to make a start as soon as possible. After saying her goodbyes, Carla walked across the car park to her car and got in. She turned on the engine and picked up a notepad from the passenger seat with the name and address of her holiday destination, she had written down earlier that day. Carla then began to enter the address into her sat-nav for her next destination. Before she left, she glanced back towards the

13

Moonraker Hotel and said to herself, *well, after all that, it is time to return to earth. I am off for two weeks away from it all, and I am looking forward to some quiet time and thinking a few things over in my head.* She glanced back at her notepad again, looking at a name she had written at the bottom of the page, *Henry Farmer,* and thought to herself, *I wonder what kind of man he is?*

The Old Mill
Chapter 2

After leaving the city of Bath, Carla was soon on the open road, driving north along the A46 towards the village of Pennsylvania. Just before reaching the village, she took a left turn into a single track country lane. The narrow lane went gently winding on downhill for about a mile, and as she proceeded the countryside became more rural and unspoilt; with a varied collection of small fields, tall old trees and overgrown hedges.

She drove through a section of woodland and a farm came into view. Carla slowed down in readiness to read any sign or plaque at the entrance of the farm, which would confirm that she had arrived at her destination.

"Oh yes, this is the place, *Prosperity Farm and Stables.*"

Also near the entrance to the farm was a small wooden stall with a hand-painted sign, which read; *free-range eggs for sale.* She looked at the stall for a few moments and thought to herself, *no eggs there today. Perhaps they have sold them all today?* She smiled to herself, knowing that her two weeks of peace and quiet in the countryside were just about to begin. Carla turned into the long farm driveway and slowed down to take in every detail of her home for the next two weeks. The driveway began with green fields on either side of it, followed on her left by a large block of stables with a white post and rail fence around

15

them. Just after the stables, there was a five-bar wooden field gate, the entrance to farm lane, which had tractor tyre marks cut into the turf. The farm lane led in a straight line directly up a long sloping field to the brow of a hill, with woodland on the left of the farm lane, and an open green pasture field on the right.

That field looks quite inviting and picturesque. I wonder what I can see from the brow of that hill.

Adjacent to farm lane was the large garden belonging to the farmhouse, surrounded by a hedge; tall enough to provide some privacy, and low enough for someone passing by to peer over. The farmhouse caught Carla's imagination immediately, with its generous proportions. It was four stories high and had a farmhouse-porch the full length of the front of the house. Directly in front of the house was a very large concrete yard which was also surrounded by a wide assortment of farm buildings. Some were in the traditional old style of red brick with oak beams, while others were more state-of-the-art modern farm buildings of steel and concrete design, but everything was spotlessly clean and tidy.

Carla turned into the right-hand corner of the yard and parked her car near an old Land Rover and an assortment of other cars. *This must be where everyone parks around here*, she thought. Carla got out of her car and walked towards the farmhouse, and then she stopped when she noticed a farm dog, a Collie, lying lazily on the front porch without a care in the world. Carla turned around to take everything in. She noticed her holiday home, *The Old Mill*. She had been so distracted by everything to her left as she drove down the driveway, that she had failed to notice her holiday home was on her right-hand side, opposite the garden of the farmhouse.

As she looked over her new home for the next two weeks, she pondered its construction. The base of the building consisted of four red brick archway tunnels. This had the effect of raising the building by another story.

Most unusual. I wonder what they were originally used for.

Looking up from there the odd design of this unique building continued with a mixture of red brick and some Oak beams here and there. *The Old Mill* directly faced the garden of the farm house. The entrance to the property was via an external steel Mezzanine staircase. The steps began on the side of the building nearest her car and then led up to a steel Mezzanine balcony along the front of the building, where two wide doors were the entry point. These timber-framed doors were stable doors by design, but with a glass panel in each section, top and bottom.

That is a very odd building. I am sure it must have had many uses in its lifetime, but I like it; something out of the ordinary to help me escape from the rat race.

The top two halves of the stable doors were open and pinned back to let the air in, giving the place a certain inviting welcome. Carla wondered if she should just go up and settle in, or if she should find Mr Henry Farmer first. She paused for a few moments to listen to the sounds around her.

First, she heard an assortment of bird song, which made her smile. Next, she heard some female voices coming from the direction of the stables, but when she looked in that direction she could not see anyone outside the stables. A few moments later Carla heard the sound of someone chopping wood with an axe.

Well, that sounds like a man at work.

As Carla continued to listen, she traced the sound to one of the traditional red brick buildings, nearest the farmhouse. She approached the small open wooden door and peered in. After her eyes adjusted from the strong sunlight to the relative darkness of the wood store, she could make out a man's figure in the low light.

He raised his axe again to split the big log in front of him. As he did so, the sharp edge of the axe caught the light and momentarily flashed brightly, and then came crashing down onto the log with such a great force splitting it in two and sending the two new halves flying away from each other in opposite directions.

This relatively simple act connected with Carla and with a little excitement in her voice, she said out loud, "Oh, you remind me of my late dad, he knew how to sharpen his axe to the point where you could see your face reflected in it's the cutting edge. And like you, he swung his axe with great precision every time."

The man spoke. She could not see him yet.

"Not everyone knows how to properly sharpen an axe, the correct way, I mean, with a stone."

His deep masculine voice contained hints of caring and tenderness within it. She liked the sound of his voice a lot. It sent a tingle down Carla's spine upon hearing it, much to her surprise.

"You must be Carla I assume, and a good timekeeper I see. I like that."

He gently swung his axe again, this time embedding it in a very big log, ready for use next time.

"I'd better come out and show you around."

Carla was surprised at how much she was drawn to his voice. The man walked slowly towards the doorway, negotiating

18

assorted chopped wooden obstacles on the floor as he walked. Carla took a few spaces back so that he could step outside easily. He emerged into the daylight.

If she was surprised to have a tingle run down her spine upon hearing his voice for the first time, then she was even more surprised upon seeing him for the first time in daylight, as she felt a flutter in her chest.

Instantly, her inner voice said to her, *you can stop that right now, Carla. He is old enough to be your father, and then some. You are not some school kid, and you have always shown better restraint before.*

"I'm Henry Farmer," he said, straightening himself up.

Carla liked everything she saw. He stood there with a strong posture and stature, wearing boots, jeans and a long-sleeved checked shirt with the sleeves rolled up. The neck of the shirt was open wide and revealed a strong well-toned muscular chest.

If you stare at his chest any longer, he'll notice what you are doing. But hey, the guys do it to us all the time, don't they?

She raised her head and looked into his face. He had a thick head of hair, a 50/50 mix of grey and dark colours. His face was handsome in a distinguished kind of way, with an overall kind and friendly presence. She looked into his eyes, which looked so beautiful and inviting, while thinking, *for an older guy you look quite amazing, even though you must be in your late fifties. I bet he is older than that, a lot older than that.*

"Come this way Carla and I will show you around *The Old Mill*. If you have a suitcase or a few bags in your car, I can carry them up the stairs for you."

"That is very kind. I only have one suitcase, but it is a bit heavy, so I would appreciate it if you took it up there for me."

They walked over to her car and Henry lifted the suitcase out of the boot. He walked to the foot of the stairs and gestured for her to go ahead of him. As she took her first few steps on the steel Mezzanine staircase, she noticed how every step gently echoed through the steelwork. As she listened to the steel staircase, her attention was drawn to a new sound. It was the bark of a small dog.

"Ah, here comes Ginger."

A small white dog came running across the yard at great speed, barking all the way. He was heading for a small gap under the garden hedge. He passed through it without slowing down and continued barking and running along the garden, before disappearing somewhere out of sight around the back of the house. Carla laughed at the little dog's performance, and then looked at the Collie dog on the front porch, who just lay there unmoved, with his head resting on his front paws.

"You will like little Ginger. He often gets to be the best of pals with the people who stay here. Especially if they give him a few treats."

"Why is he called Ginger, isn't he all white?"

"Yes, he is nearly all white, apart from a small tan patch on one of his ears. When he arrived here as a puppy, a little boy was staying here with his mother, and when he saw the little dog, he kept talking about his ginger ear. So the name stuck, even though the dog's ears are tan coloured and not ginger at all."

At the top of the stairs, she asked, "What is your other dog called."

"Max, but most people around here call him 'Lazy dog' because he just lies down all day and only moves when he wants to eat something, but that's another story."

Carla turned left, and walked a short way along the steel balcony and entered *The Old Mill* with Henry carrying her suitcase close behind her.

Compared to the outside of *The Old Mill*, the inside was very modern and contemporary, although a little compact. Standing just inside the glass double barn-door doorway, directly in front of her was a large sofa, perfectly placed to watch the world go by. Behind the sofa was the entrance to the bedroom with an en suite bathroom. On her left was a very compact cooking area, and on her right was a bookcase with a wide assortment of books on it. There was a small coffee table in front of the sofa with a pair of binoculars on it and a book with a colourful cover entitled, *Pocket Guide to British Birds.*

"I think I am going to be alright here, and I must say that everywhere looks very clean and tidy."

"Oh, I don't deserve any thanks for that. I have a very helpful lady from the village who does that for me. She puts everything in order ready for each new holiday-maker's arrival. She always does such a good job, no one has ever complained. I am so lucky to have her around. I really am. I don't know what I would do without her."

"Could you put my case in the bedroom for me, please? That must be the most logical place for it, so I can unpack it." Henry slipped his boots off, "We don't want me to mess the nice clean floor now, do we?"

Carla smiled. "No, of course not."

21

He carried her suitcase to the bedroom and Carla followed him to take a closer look at the room.

"Oh, this looks like a nice and cosy room."

"Yes indeed, but oddly enough many people who stop here on their own appear to like sleeping on the sofa too. I am not sure why that is."

A brief moment of silence fell between them as she pondered the oddity of standing in a bedroom with a handsome man who was almost a stranger to her

Don't even think about it Carla, you have only just arrived.

She returned to the living room and Henry followed. For the next few minutes, Henry showed Carla around the fixtures and fittings of *The Old Mill* and when he was happy that she knew her way around the place and how everything worked, he said, "You should have a great couple of weeks here. You have certainly picked the best two weeks for the weather; apparently the heatwave of the past fortnight is predicted to become even hotter from tomorrow."

"That is what they are saying alright. The next two weeks are supposed to be the highest temperatures of the year."

"According to Kirra, she is one of the ladies around here, this heatwave is going to end with the mother-of-all storms, and out of a clear sky too."

Henry smiled to himself and chuckled a little, and then added, "Kirra is a bit eccentric, a wonderful soul, don't get me wrong, but a bit eccentric in some people's eyes. Actually, despite what many think of her, she is quite a clever lady. She used to be a history teacher until she became disillusioned with it. She is someone you are bound to meet around here sooner or later. She

22

usually has a pair of dowsing-rods in her hands, or divining-rods, as some people call them. Either way, you can't miss her."

"So, the mother-of-all storms is coming, and out of a clear sky too. That will be something to see."

"It certainly will. Oh, that reminds me, I must apologise for the lack of air conditioning. When the old unit gave up the ghost, I ordered a new one straight away, but unfortunately, it has not been installed yet. I will spare you the full details because it is a long tale-of-troubles, which should never have happened. It is quite amazing to see the way some people try to run their businesses. Basic things like customer satisfaction, and doing what you say you are going to do, are just bizarre concepts to some of them!" He shrugged. "The last person to hire *The Old Mill* was another person that liked to sleep on the sofa too, she said to me, 'With the bedroom window open, and the tops of the front stable doors open, it provided a nice steady breeze.' But that was her. She never used the bed once apparently."

"Don't worry about the air-conditioning, Henry. I'll be alright. If not, the open windows and the sofa might be an option. There is only me here and I sleep well, anyway."

Her inner voice teased, *you liked saying his name, didn't you?*

"What are you planning to do with your holiday, any plans?"

"Not much really, I want to chill out and relax. Get away from the rat race for a bit and begin to think a few things through. I feel as if I have lost my direction in life a bit these past few years. Although, there is one thing I am planning to do, and that's a bit of drawing. I used to be good at it back in school."

"What type of subjects do you like to draw?"

"Anything natural, trees, birds, landscapes, that kind of thing. I've never been any good at drawing people, and I find it especially hard to draw hands."

"Well, you are very welcome to go about the farm anywhere you choose to find suitable subjects to draw, make yourself at home."

"Thank you, that is very kind."

Henry raised his arm and pointed towards the top of the field behind his house and garden, "If you go through the gate near the stable block and walk up the farm lane towards the brow of the hill you will arrive at that large fallen tree up there."

"Oh yes, I see it. The big old one, lying across your lane."

"That's the one. Later in the year when I have more free time, I will have to go up there with my chain-saw and saw it up for firewood, but for now, there it stays. It might make a nice spot for you to sit down on the trunk, and draw away to your heart's content. The last lady to stay here would sit in that old tree for hours with binoculars in hand and that book of birds over there on the table, or Ornithology as it's called. She loved it up there in that tree. Those old trees attract quite an array of birdlife if you like that sort of thing."

"That spot should suit me very nicely. I will check it out. I was brought up on my late father's farm. Happy times, which unfortunately came to an end much too early. So, I will really enjoy being here on the farm again."

Henry gave Carla a sympathetic look upon hearing about her late father.

"Well, I'll leave you to settle in."

He went outside and picked up his boots, "I'll put these back on at the bottom of the staircase, a bit easier that way."

24

Then he gave Carla a very pleasant smile. "Oh, by the way, I should have said you are very welcome to use the swimming pool and hot tub too."

"I didn't know there was a pool and hot tub here."

"Oh yes, there is." Henry stood a little to the side so that Carla could see them in Henry's garden. "Too many people work too hard, it is important to have a few treats and enjoy life along the way, don't you agree?"

Carla stepped forward to take a better look at Henry's garden. Nearest the house was a very large patio with an assortment of garden tables and chairs and several luxurious sunbeds. At the far end of the patio stood the biggest barbeque she had ever seen, near that was a very large, expensive hot tub near it. Between the patio and the garden hedge, nearest to the farm lane, was a medium-sized open-air swimming pool. On the other side of all this, just before the long field which sloped away from the house, was a well-kept lawn. Carla viewed it all with keen interest and gave Henry a nod of approval with a happy smile.

He appeared pleased that she liked all that she saw, and then said, "Barbeque tonight, around 7:30. Please come along and meet everyone. "You can hear and smell the barbeque from up here, so you might as well be part of it."

"I suppose you are right about that, so why not?"

"Have you drunk much homemade cider before?"

"Oh yes, loads. My dear old dad was something of an expert in making it with apples from our orchard."

Henry looked pleased, "Great, it is good to have people around who appreciate a good drop of homemade cider or scrumpy as we like to call it. Tonight, those that want to can sample my latest batch. But be warned it is very strong, so be sure to eat plenty first, we don't want you getting drunk now do we?"

Carla laughed off Henry's caution dismissively, "Oh, you don't need to worry about me, I can handle my drink."

"Glad to hear it, Carla, a girl after my own heart. Well, we will see you later on then."

He gave her a warm and friendly smile and then walked away with the accompanying rumble and echo from the steel staircase. Carla went back inside and smiled as she surveyed the pleasant room, and then happily said, "Holiday time, just wonderful."

She perused some of the book titles on the bookcase. There was a wide range of books, everything from romantic fiction to somewhat more practical titles like *Captain Scott* by Ranulph Fiennes, and *Think and Grow Rich,* by Napoleon Hill. She removed *Think and Grow Rich* from the bookshelf and looked at it more closely, then quietly said, "I've heard about this book a few times before, but I have never read it."

She opened the cover to find a few handwritten words inside it:

To Henry. Thanks for everything. Love Judith.

This put an amused smile on her face.

"I wonder who Judith was."

After looking it over she was about to return it to the bookshelf when a thought entered her mind, *put it on the table beside the Pocket Guide to British Birds book, and be sure to read it.*

Carla sighed because she hadn't been planning to read anything during the holiday and she certainly did not feel like reading much, anyway. She placed the book on the table and somehow felt like she had just done the right thing. Over the years she had learnt to trust her inner voice because it had proven to be right so many times before. She also appreciated her inner voice because it was a positive force in her life and because she had heard of many people not as lucky as her whose inner voices had, tormented them, belittled them, and ridiculed them, sometimes almost to the point of suicide. She had occasionally wondered if the inner voice was something that had to be trained, or did you simply get what you are given? However she was content in the knowledge that her inner voice was a very good thing to have alongside her in life.

Just then, her mobile phone rang. Carla picked it up and looked at the screen to see who it was. The words, *Lying Lynn* were on the display. Seeing the call was from her friend Lynn put a smirk on her face. As soon as she answered it, Lynn spoke in a loud, enthusiastic voice, "Hi there, it's the honest journalist. Yes, your old friend, Lying Lynn. Guess what, guess what?"

"Well…"

"No, too slow you old snail. So, I am going to have to tell you myself. Well, Wilson is now officially my best mate in the whole wide world. Well, sort of. Do you know what he has let me have?"

"First chance of having a love child with him? Just as you wanted."

"F-off, don't be facetious, darling. I don't know how anyone could be so rude, honestly," she said mockingly with pretend seriousness.

"Go on then please tell me what it is, I assume that it is some big newsworthy story if you are this excited."

"Sophie Archer."

"Wow, the actress."

"Yes, Sophie, Minnie Mouse, Archer."

"Sophie Archer, sometimes called, Sophie, Minnie Mouse, Archer, because she is nearly always wearing either an item of Minnie Mouse clothing or jewellery."

"That's her. There is even a rumour that she has a very small Minnie Mouse tattoo somewhere on her body, but only a very few personally selected people would ever get the chance to see it. Know what I mean?"

"Now Lynn, stop thinking like a journalist."

"She likes to wear red a lot too. Anyway, according to Wilson, Sophie is being a bit of a naughty girl right now, and the man in her life isn't going to like that much when it all hits the fan."

"Is that where you come in?"

"But of course darling, someone has to do it, so it might as well be me. According to Wilson, twenty-two-year-old Sophie Archer, widely regarded as an exceptional British actress, the darling of film and social media, who as we all know is engaged to be married later this year to that equally well-known big American Hollywood actor, has just recently secretly added another man to her life. A man from the Bath area and he is a much older guy than her too. Not much more is known about him, or the affair for that matter, making it my job to find out every little grubby detail, for the greater public good of course."

"But of course. Actually, I quite like her as an actress, so please be kind to her."

"Kind, you say? Hum? Well, I could tell her story in a kind way. Kind of truthful, kind of fully revealed, kind of fully exposed with everything laid bare."

"You are awful, you know that, don't you?"

"Oh yes, dear. I try to be, but I am just doing my job, dear, after all."

"Don't be too hard on her. Other than that, I am very pleased for you, sounds like just the story you have been searching for."

"Oh yes, it is an absolutely huge story for me. The only small problem is, right now no one appears to know exactly where she. But, I do know that she has to be in her makeup trailer very early tomorrow morning, getting ready for an early morning film shoot."

"Where are they filming?"

"Sophie is filming on location in Bath as luck would have it; some period piece film, with quite a few other big films, stars appearing in it too. All this has worked out very well for me because I have always wanted to stay at the Moonraker Hotel in Bath. So I've booked myself in for a few nights. Perfect for me really. I get to cover the Sophie Archer story, I get a few nights in the Moonraker, and with the floating stones here, I might find out a bit more about those too."

"Are they still up, the stones I mean?"

"Oh yes, and I must say those floating stones are simply amazing to watch. Quite fascinating. I know that some of my colleagues are trying to find out more about them, but there is a lot of secrecy surrounding them. I might have an advantage over them, staying here. Imagine what a double scoop it would be, finding out everything about, Sophie Archer, and the Moonraker's floating stones. We will have to see what happens. Anyway, I'll settle for Sophie right now, wherever she is."

Lynn paused, and then moved on to a new subject, "So anyway, have you found a tree to hug yet?"

"Sorry to disappoint you, but I am not planning to hug any trees."

"It's the denial. I think that is the worst part of it. Don't worry. Go hug your trees, I'll keep your secret... for now. How is your room, or barn, or whatever it is?"

"As I told you, I am staying at *The Old Mill,* and it is quite beautiful and peaceful."

"That's good," Lynn said without any real interest, "quite beautiful and peaceful you say?"

"Yes, and I have just met the owner, Henry Farmer."

There was a pause from Lynn because the journalist inside her spotted a little something, then she enquired, "Tell me more about Henry Farmer."

Carla cleared her throat and quietly said, "Well, there is not much to say about him."

"Not much to say about him. Really? Well, how about you describe him to me, to begin with."

"Okay, well, I suppose he is in his late fifties."

"I see, so he must be in his early sixties then."

"Well, I suppose he might be. I'm not sure because he is quite a well-kept and attractive guy, for an older guy I mean."

"Could you define attractive for me, please?"

Carla cleared her throat again, "Well, he has something about him."

Carla was quiet for a few moments. She was very surprised by how much describing Henry affected her. A man she had just met.

"Now, now Carla, take a deep breath, and then tell me the truth about this guy."

Carla took a deep breath, held on to it, and then let it out and began talking again, "Oh wow, I can't believe I am saying this. Henry is amazing. He really does have that X factor, that something special that makes him stand out from the crowd. Yes, I suppose that he might well be in his sixties, if I am honest, but it is more than just a man simply growing distinguished with age. A look, an attractiveness that must have been with him all of his life, he's got it, that X factor that only the lucky few have."

"Oh my, oh my, I can see the headline in the Sunday papers now, *Holiday Romance with OAP.*" Then she laughed at her friend's expense, as Carla protested, "No, no, it's nothing like that."

Lynn was laughing too much to continue talking, and so she said goodbye to Carla through the laughter and rang off.

Carla found herself quite amused by her semi-confession and Lynn's reaction to it. Then with a smile and the odd chuckle to herself, she picked up the binoculars and walked out onto the balcony and looked about her without too much thought.

A young lady with long blonde hair, wearing a red bikini walked out of the farmhouse and began to relax on one of the sunbeds. Carla then noticed two horses and their riders coming over the brow of the hill in the distance, she held up her binoculars to take a better look at the two horses.

She noticed how the two female horse riders were chatting away like old friends, happy and relaxed in each other's company. Carla thought that they looked to be in their mid to late thirties.

She lowered the binoculars again and looked towards the stables, where she could see some young ladies busy in various stable activities. A lady wearing a light blue, long summer dress walked out of one of the stables and sat on a straw bale outside. She looked around thirty years old and quite unhappy. Her light blue dress looked out of place because everyone else at the stables was wearing trousers, or jodhpurs for practical reasons. Her hair was kept in an untidy ponytail.

As Carla observed her from a distance, she noticed how the lady began to rock, back and forth, to comfort herself as she sat on the bale of straw.

"That's not a good sign," Carla quietly said.

She looked back towards the house. The Collie dog was still lazily resting on the same spot.

"No change there then."

Returning her attention to the lady in the garden lying on the sunbed, who now appeared to be reading some notes from a folder, she thought, *Henry appears to be the only man here.* Her inner voice added in observation, *or to put it another way, Henry is surrounded by ladies, of which you are one.*

Carla pondered this for a moment and then dismissed it as an odd passing thought. Then something on the cover of the folder, the girl in the red bikini was reading from, as she lay on the sunbed, caught Carla's eye. She discreetly raised her binoculars again to observe it. As she adjusted the binoculars, and the cover of the folder came into clear view, which showed an image of Minnie Mouse. Carla slowly lowered the binoculars again as she began to speculate about what she might just have seen.

Henry walked into the garden from the house with a glass of orange juice, which he held out for the young lady. She sat up

32

and took it from him, and then chatted. From these few subtle movements, Carla instantly recognised who she was because Carla had seen this lady many times before, at the cinema. Henry Farmer was in his garden with the film star Sophie Archer.

Barbeque Night
Chapter 3

Carla unpacked and soon settled in. With nothing especially to do, she sat on the sofa and began reading the book from the bookcase she had picked up earlier, *Think and Grow Rich,* by Napoleon Hill. Carla began by looking through the table of contents, which fired her imagination. She read chapter one, the introduction to the book. After reading the first paragraph, she paused to reflect on it, and then read it again aloud.

Truly, "thoughts are things," and powerful things at that,
when they are mixed with definiteness of purpose,
persistence, and a burning desire for their translation into riches,
or other material objects.

"I think this is just the right book for me to read right now." She happily read on, often pausing to reflect on something she had just read. When she had read most of chapter one, she became distracted by the faint sound of a distant bell ringing. It sounded almost like a church bell, and yet somehow it didn't. She looked at her watch, "Oh, five-thirty already."

As the bell continued with its rhythmical chimes Carla pondered, "Surely, there can't be a church service at this time of day?"

Curious, she stood up and walked onto the balcony, as she did so the rhythmical ringing appeared to quicken its pace. She looked to the horizon, in the direction she thought the sound was emanating from, but couldn't see any suitable building that could be responsible for producing it. Then the rhythmical ringing became quite random and almost chaotic before coming to an abrupt end.

I wonder what that was. She waited a few moments, for the ringing bell to begin again, but nothing happened. She looked into the garden. Sophie's sunbed was now empty.

It is a hot day. Film stars can't have too much sun on their delicate skin, I suppose. She returned to the sofa to finish chapter one of her book.

Around quarter-past-seven Carla left *The Old Mill* leaving the top of the barn-doors open to help keep the rooms cool. She wanted a quiet word with Henry and she knew that he was alone at the moment, as he prepared the barbeque. As she approached him, he cheerfully called out to her, "Hello there. All settled in I hope?"

"Yes, thanks. I wanted to talk to you about something."

Henry gave her a very pleasant easy smile, "I thought that you did. You have an odd glint in your eye and a slightly embarrassing smirk of a smile, and you almost appear amused about something too. So, please go ahead and speak, I'm curious to know what it is."

"Sophie Archer," Carla said quietly.

"Oh, you spotted her, didn't you?"

Carla grinned. "Oh yes, anyway, please forgive me because it is none of my business anyway, but I have seen a few of her films, and I very much like her as an actress, so I wish her well, I really do."

"Go on."

35

Carla lost the grin and got to the point, "Well, I have a friend who is a journalist, well sort of a friend anyway."

Keen-eyed Henry knew how to read people and soon spotted that Carla and the journalist did not have a perfect friendship. "She is not your best friend in the whole wide world, is she?"

Carla shook her head in agreement, "No, not really, she has many good qualities, although she hides them well most of the time. My friendship with her is a particularly long and complicated story that is best left for another time," Carla paused. "Anyway, the thing is this, I understand from her that she is investigating Sophie Archer at the moment and planning to write a sensational story about her and her love life. So, could you please tell her to be very careful what she does in Bath, because there is a journalist intent on watching her every move?"

Carla realised that she was now looking Henry directly in the eye. Immediately after speaking, she diverted her gaze away from him because his eyes were just so captivating.

I could stare into his eyes for hours, so I must look away, or else he might think that I am interested in him.

Henry then, very quietly and with genuine appreciation said, "Thank you, Carla, she is inside at the moment and has a lot of lines to learn, ready for an early film shoot tomorrow morning. I will have a word with her and pass on what you have told me."

"Good, I wouldn't like to think of her being hurt by a news story that I might have been able to help prevent."

"She loves him very much, you know, that American actor of hers, and Sophie is looking forward to getting married to him. But, well, you know, sometimes a girl just wants to live a little first."

Henry was about to say a bit more, but Carla prevented him.

"Please don't tell me anything more, it is none of my business, really it isn't."

"Well, thanks again, it was very kind and thoughtful sharing that with me. I am sure Sophie will very much appreciate the tip-off too. Come on let me get you a drink. Would you like to try some of my homemade cider?"

"Oh yes, please. A nice bit of scrumpy would be perfect."

They walked over to a small table, which was set up with assorted drinks and glasses. Carla noticed that amongst the various drinking glasses there was a set of six with two red dice on them. As she looked closer, she discovered that the red dice had white hearts on them instead of white dots.

I wonder if they were a present from one of his female friends, she pondered.

As Henry poured her a glass of cider from a small old wooden barrel, she was thinking about his aftershave. Carla had never before found an aftershave quite so captivating. She had not noticed it earlier, so he must have put it on when getting ready for the evening.

She couldn't help it, she had to ask, "Please forgive me asking Henry, but your aftershave is quite something. What is it?"

"Oh yes, I love it too, it is an exceptionally good one. Unfortunately, I can't tell you the name, because it doesn't have one, but I can tell you that it came from Spain. A lady friend of mine, (shall we say) and a lovely lady too, she was from Spain. Her family owned a perfume-house over there, and one day she gave me a little bottle of scent and said, "I made this just for you, think of me whenever you wear it."

"It is certainly something special."

Carla couldn't resist inhaling a bit more, "Oh, wow."

"Unfortunately, there is not much left in the bottle now. I'll miss it when it's gone."

Henry handed Carla a glass of his cider, "Here you are, try this and enjoy."

"It looks lovely, just like my dear old dad used to make."

She drank some down, "Cider is the perfect refreshing drink in hot weather."

"They say that tomorrow will be the start of even hotter days as this heatwave continues."

Just then, two female voices spoke almost in unison, "Hello Henry."

Henry looked pleased to see them. They both walked up to Henry on either side of him and kissed him on each cheek. It was all done in a very casual and familiar manner. Clearly, these three were very good old friends.

"Ladies, let me introduce you to Carla, she is staying at *The Old Mill* for the next couple of weeks."

"Did I see you two on horseback earlier this afternoon, coming over the brow of the hill?"

"Yes, that was us, nice to meet you, Carla, I'm Tracy.

"And I am Fiona, nice to meet you too."

"Could I ask you two lovely ladies to look after Carla for me, and make sure that she doesn't get too tipsy, and keep her out of mischief too, please," Henry said light-heartedly.

Tracy gave a friendly smile and said, "No problem Henry, but anyone who can drink your homemade cider must be able to handle their drink quite well."

And Fiona added, "Henry, a little bit of mischief never hurt anyone, anyway."

"Carla, I must warn you about these two. They are a real comic duo," Henry teased. "Tracy is the straight-man of this duo (or rather the woman in her case) and Fiona delivers the gags, or one-liners, usually with a bit of innuendo too. You will enjoy yourself with these two. Sometimes they make a trio when Stephany joins in too. Stephany has a wonderful dry, sarcastic humour, she is very entertaining."

An hour later, and after a few glasses of scrumpy along with some excellent barbeque food, Carla was sat opposite Tracy and Fiona at one of the garden tables, laughing and joking and having a good time with them.

It was a hot summers evening, and Henry's barbeque party had a very pleasant atmosphere about it. Music played from a good stereo system, and plenty of people had turned up, most of which were enjoying themselves in good conversation combined with plenty of eating and drinking, and a few were cooling off in the swimming pool with a drink in their hands.

Tracy looked around her and commented, "You have to hand it to Henry he does put on a great barbeque, every time."

Fiona, replied, "Oh yes, he is good at putting on a barbeque. In fact, I would go so far as to say that Henry is good at everything, isn't he Tracy?"

Before Tracy could respond Stephany arrived, suddenly taking the empty chair at the end of the table, with her plate landing heavily on the table, "Oh yes, Henry is very good at everything, indeed he is."

She said with a smirk on her face. Tracy enquired, "Aren't you hot wearing that leather waistcoat of yours?"

39

"Nonsense, it is never too hot for wearing my stylish leather waistcoat."

Carla thought to herself, *you must be quite hot wearing, long boots, jeans, a button blouse and that leather waistcoat. It is a nice look though.*

Stephany shook her head of long wavy blonde hair, flaunting it as if to make some kind of statement.

Tracy politely said, "Oh Stephany, I hope my hair is as great as yours when I am your age."

Fiona, never one to miss her chance of using a one-liner, teased Stephany, "Oh yes, when I am fifty-five I want a wig just like yours."

Playing Fiona's game Stephany teased her back, "Wig indeed. Fiona all I can say to you is, be careful what you wish for. As for me, my beautiful blonde locks are the real thing. You little girls can only dream of looking as good as me in fifteen years."

With a serious expression, Stephany looked closely at her plate of food, which consisted of only one item; a very large beef burger in a bun, with salad and a burger sauce.

Tracy enquired, "Is everything okay with your food Stephany?" Fiona added, "I know that look, you are worried about something."

Still, with a serious expression on her face, Stephany said, "Well, Henry is an amazing guy on the barbeque. I know he is, but," she paused, "it's, just that I haven't seen Marie's horse for a while."

Realising the joke Tracy and Fiona giggled, and then Tracy commented, "that's not really fair is it, Stephany?"

Stephany pretended to look hurt by Tracy's words, while Fiona added, "Anyway, while she might not actually have a horse at the moment, she does have an amazing saddle."

Fiona paused for effect to deliver her punch line, "I know that Henry is very impressed with her saddle."

These three friends all giggled at their shared private joke, which left Carla wondering who Marie, the lady with no horse was, but before she could ask Stephany enquired, "So who have we here?"

"I am Carla. I am here on holiday for the next two weeks, staying in *The Old Mill.*"

"Looks like we have competition girls," Fiona said.

"Competition for what," Carla enquired.

"Oh please, don't pretend you don't know," Stephany said dryly with a strained smile.

Carla shook her head, and then Stephany continued after a slight chuckle to herself, "Well, my dear Carla, if you are staying here for two weeks, you will fall into Henry's arms, and helplessly give in to him."

"They always do," Tracy added with honesty.

"Sorry to disappoint you, but I don't see him that way. I have to admit he is one amazing guy, especially for his age. Somehow, he is strangely attractive, but no, that isn't going to happen."

Fiona added, "Well I have never seen any lady staying at *The Old Mill* on her own deny herself."

Tracy added, "They always do."

"Oh don't worry, we are used to having to share Henry. He will never belong to one woman exclusively," Stephany said dryly, "We all get our turn in the end."

Carla swirled her empty glass in her hand and tried to use a little humour to change the subject.

"This cider must be very strong, for it must be responsible for me imagining the in-delicate discussion you ladies are having about, poor old charming Henry."

The ladies all chuckled upon hearing the term, *poor old charming Henry.*

"I have enjoyed four glasses of Henry's wonderful homemade scrumpy so far, but it is probably time to move onto some other drink."

"You've had four glasses of scrumpy, more like six of them," Fiona said.

Stephany decidedly stated, "Well, anyone who can drink four to six glasses of Henry's fine cider must be a good drinker, and only a good drinker can tackle a few glasses of Henry's other very fine drink, *Red Tractor Diesel.*"

"What is, *Red Tractor Diesel*? Surely it can't be as the name implies tractor fuel straight out of the farm's red diesel tank?"

Stephany jumped out of her chair, "One bottle of *Red Tractor Diesel* coming up."

And off she walked in Henry's direction to find a bottle. Tracy looked at Carla reassuringly.

"Don't worry, it only looks like red diesel. It is more of a blended mix of homemade damson red wine and vodka, but it is quite strong though."

Carla nodded her head in approval, "Sounds okay to me. I'll try anything once."

"You'll try anything once. Once you try Henry, once will not be enough," Fiona teased.

Carla laughed it off.

"Anyway, moving on. I was wondering who is Marie, the lady with no horse?"

Tracy said with some feeling, "Oh, that's a sad story. She is the lady you will see around here who usually looks quite sad because a few years ago she lost her husband."

"Is she the lady in the long light blue dress? She looks around thirty."

"Yes, that's her. Unlike the rest of us, she can wear a dress around here because she doesn't have a horse to look after. Isn't that right, Fiona?"

"Yes, it is true, she doesn't own a horse, but she does rent a stable from Henry. Marie always claims that she is in the market for a horse, but I don't think that she will ever buy one. I am not altogether sure if she can even ride."

Tracy added, "She does have a very good saddle, though."

"It's a bit of a standing joke around here. Marie's saddle is quite amazing. You definitely need to see it, because it is the very best saddle that you will ever set your eyes on."

"Why is that, what makes it so special?"

Tracy leaned in a little closer, "Because the only thing she actually does around here, is polish that saddle."

Carla thought for a moment, "So if I've got this right. Marie does not actually own a horse, and quite possibly never will, but she pays out for stable hire just so she can polish a saddle that she may never actually use. Correct?" Tracy and Fiona nodded in agreement.

"Why does she do that?"

"Henry," they both said quietly in unison. Tracy then added, "Because she wants to be here, near Henry."

43

"I don't know whether to believe you two sometimes. You talk as if everyone wants to bed Henry."

Fiona leaned closer and said in a hushed tone, "They do. And although she might not look like it, Marie is the worst one here, her appetite for..." Fiona paused, "Well, it is like this you see, she lost her man. I truly believed that they loved each other, and they were absolutely devoted to each other, but one day he disappeared. No one knows for sure what happened to him, but I think it is fair to say that through no fault of his own his days were cut short. Some person or organisation decided that he had to be silenced or taken out of the picture, but that is another story. Since then, Marie has been a girl who moves through cycles. Most of the time she acutely feels the loss of her man and looks very unhappy, then slowly over a period of a few weeks she gradually brightens up and lets her hair down. When she feels like her old self again, she makes a play for Henry and parties with him like some wild untamed animal. Honestly, Marie is the wildest girl here, no doubt about it. When she really gets going, she makes the rest of us feel like nuns. Then after a few days of the wildest debauchery imaginable, the guilt sets in and she returns to the beginning of the cycle again: guilt, loneliness and sorrow. She is still technically married, and she truly loves her husband, wherever he is, or whatever happened to him. Many of us here have tried to get her some professional help, but Marie just seems stuck in this rut of endless cycles at the moment."

Tracy added, "It's true, I've seen it happen many times before with Marie. I think at the moment she is improving day by day, so some truly wild times are not far away. It is quite a transformation to behold, believe me, she becomes so free and loses all of her inhibitions."

44

"Wow, that is quite something, but it sounds like a sad tale really."

They both nodded in agreement.

Just then Stephany returned with two bottles of *Red Tractor Diesel* and caused a much-needed change in the conversation.

"Here you are girls, two bottles and four glasses."

Tracy enquired, "I thought you said you were going to collect one bottle of Red Tractor Diesel?"

Fiona quickly spoke on Stephany's behalf, "She did get just one bottle, one bottle in each hand."

Stephany grunted in agreement and said, "Oh yes, and Henry asked if we are all having a good time."

The bottles and the glasses landed heavily on the table.

Stephany asked Carla, "Can you see now why it is called, *Red Tractor Diesel*?"

"Yes I can, in colour and general appearance, it would be hard to tell it apart from *Red Tractor Diesel.* I just hope that it tastes and smells better than the fuel that is poured into a tractor's fuel tank."

"Well Carla, you will soon find out for yourself," Stephany filled a glass and gave it to Carla, saying, "Cheers."

Carla took a large sip and savoured its flavours before swallowing it down.

"Well, there is nothing wrong with that, a little bit dry I grant you, but a good drink nonetheless. I would be happy to drink that all evening."

As Stephany began to fill the other three glasses, Tracy said to Carla with an anxious expression on her face, "Please be careful Carla, that is strong stuff and you have had a few glasses of scrumpy too."

Fiona brushed Tracy's concerns aside, "Take no notice of her, Carla. Us girls will look after you. And if you do get accidentally drunk, then I am sure that we three girls can carry you back to *The Old Mill* and tuck you into bed."

Carla briefly wondered if these three girls were now trying to get her drunk intentionally, to take some kind of advantage of her.

This must have shown on Carla's face and Stephany who said in her usual dry sarcastic tone of voice, "Don't flatter yourself, darling. It isn't going to happen." To which, they all laughed.

An hour and a half passed by very quickly as the four laughed and joked together on all kinds of unrelated topics. They emptied the first two bottles of *Red Tractor Diesel,* and they had just started a third.

There was an occasional splash of water coming toward them from the direction of the swimming pool as a growing number of people frolicked around in it.

Carla was now feeling like she had drunk quite a lot, but believed that she could still take some more even though her thoughts and reactions were clearly slowing down. Carla remembered the sound of the ringing bell that she had heard that afternoon.

"I thought I heard a bell ringing this afternoon. It sounded a bit like a church bell. Where would that sound have come from?"

The other three girls exchanged glances between each other, smiles and smirks showed on their faces, and then they burst out laughing.

"No, really, I was curious. Where does that ringing come from?"

The other three now laughed even more.

"Oh, you lot have had too much, *Tractor Red*, I mean *Tractor fuel*," she paused to recollect her thoughts, "Oh, this stuff is strong. I meant to say; you lot have had too much *Red Tractor Diesel*."

"Perhaps we should tell her," Tracy said helpfully.

Fiona added playfully, "You are right."

With a beaming smile, which meant that she was making something up, she said, "well, as I understand it. It is the ringing sound from a ghost ship, from, ye old Bristol town, or city as it is now known. Legend has it that many centuries ago when all the men of Bristol were abroad fighting for king and country, these fighting men found themselves in need of women's company to help them through the night, to help ease away the stresses and strains of a soldiers day. The king ordered that all the buxom virgin wenches of Bristol town be put on a ship and sent to the solders, so far away."

Tracy laughed aloud at her friend's made-up story, but Fiona carried on undeterred.

"They found fifty buxom virgin wenches in Bristol town and packed them tightly into a ship's hold. Unfortunately, here my tale takes a sad turn. You see, this was such a long time ago, and at that time ships did not have a Plimsoll-line, to prevent a ship from being overloaded. No sooner had the ship reached the Bristol-Channel, when it sank, and all souls were lost. They say that sometimes when the wind is blowing from the Bristol direction, you can hear the ghostly sound of the ship's bell and the faint screams of its drowning cargo."

Fiona paused and tried to keep a serious face, but soon burst out laughing at her own tall-tale and the others all burst out laughing too.

Stephany added in her usual dry, sarcastic manner, "You see that story sounded quite plausible up until the point where you mentioned finding fifty virgins in Bristol. It was all quite unbelievable after that."

This tale caused the four a great deal of laughter as they drank down even more *Red Tractor Diesel*.

Carla was feeling worse for drinking and she was struggling to hear her new friends and get her own words out clearly, "Anyway, getting back to my question, tell me about the bells."

Tracy asked, "Are you okay, Carla? You have drunk a lot more than the rest of us. Shall I get you a coffee or a glass of water?"

"Ah, she is fine," said Fiona.

"That's right, you are fine aren't you Carla," agreed Stephany, "But you have asked about the ringing bells, we should try to answer this for her."

Stephany asked Tracy with a knowing smile on her face and in an inquiring tone of voice, as if she already knew the answer to her question, "Tracy, have you ever heard these bells?"

Tracy's expression looked a mixture of amused and slightly embarrassed. Fiona tried to add to Tracy's awkward moment by saying, "Yes Tracy, have you ever heard these bells? It sounds like there must be more than one bell. Please, could you tell us more?"

Carla could now feel the drink was taking a hold of her, she was beginning to struggle to remain conscious, her body felt heavy and her eyelids kept trying to close. Even so, as she struggled to stay aware, she noticed how much Fiona and Stephany were enjoying teasing Tracy.

"Well, I have heard that there are actually three bells," Tracy said with a guilty smile.

Fiona enquiringly added, "Oh really, three bells you say. How would you tell them apart?"

"Well, each bell is a little louder than the other and has a slightly different ring to it."

Fiona quickly added, "Oh, each bell is a little louder and has a different ring, did you hear that Stephany? So, Tracy would it be fair to say that these bells are on different levels (so to speak), and some sound louder than others, bells on different levels, yes?"

"Yes," Tracy shyly confessed.

Fiona changed to a slightly more confessional tone of voice, "If I am honest, I think that I may have heard the bell on level one, and the bell on level two occasionally, but I don't think that I have ever heard the third bell that you talk of. Have you experienced that third bell, Stephany?"

"No, I can't say that I have. Tell us more about the third bell Tracy. For example, were you alone when you heard it."

"No," said Tracy shyly. Stephany teased Tracy still more, "Well, who was with you Tracy? Who heard the third bell with you Tracy?"

Tracy cleared her throat, "Well, I think it was Henry who heard the third bell with me."

"Oh, so you think, Henry was with you at the time and you both experienced the third bell together?"

Tracy grinned from ear to ear, and then excitedly exclaimed while waving her arms victoriously, "Yes, I've experienced the third bell with Henry."

After that, the three fell about into fits of laughter.

Carla listened as best she could to all of this, but none of it made any sense to her. As she tried to think about it, she slipped into a drunken sleep of sorts, right where she sat. For the next few hours, Carla slept with her head resting upon her crossed arms, until she was awakened by a large amount of water from the swimming pool, which somehow landed across her back. She reluctantly straightened herself back up and tried to focus her eyes, which brought Tracy into view.

"I hope you are alright. We thought it was best to let you sleep it off a bit."

Carla was still quite drunk and said nothing before returning her head to her crossed arms on the table. A few more hours passed, then she gradually became aware of loud music.

Carla thought to herself, *I recognise that old song,* it is, - *Because the Night,* by Patti Smith. The song was played a second time, but this time around it was played even louder. As she lay there Carla listened to the lyrics of the song.

> *Take me now, baby here as I am*
> *Pull me close, try and understand*
> *Desire is hunger is the fire I breathe*
> *Love is the banquet on which we feed*

Slowly she sat up and was surprised to see that Marie, the lady in the blue dress, was now sitting opposite her.

With a sympathetic look, she said, "Time for you to go bed now, Carla."

Carla looked about her with strained, tired eyes. It was now well after midnight, quite dark, and almost everyone had gone home. As she focused her eyes on the last few remaining people, all of whom were now enthusiastically dancing together to the song, she saw, Tracy, Fiona and Stephany, flaunting themselves all over Henry and dancing most seductively.

Around these four danced a lady in a long flowing red dress. She was also caught up in the lyrics of the song and was using an empty beer bottle for a pretend microphone which she used to sing along to this old classic song. Then Carla recognised the lady in the long flowing red dress, it was the actress Sophie Archer.

Carla was feeling too rough to take in anything else, so she lowered her head again to sleep as she listened to the chorus of the song.

Because the night belongs to lovers
Because the night belongs to lust
Because the night belongs lovers
Because the night belongs to us

The Day After the Night Before
Chapter 4

When Carla woke up the next morning, her head was throbbing and her body was heavy, making it difficult to make any movement.

She tried to open her eyes, but even that simple task required a number of attempts. When she eventually opened them, the room was spinning so fast that she couldn't figure out where she was.

Oh no, never again, she thought.

A few minutes later, she tried again and managed to keep her eyes open this time. She was lying on the sofa in *The Old Mill,* and still dressed as the night before.

Still dressed, that is probably a good sign. Someone must have brought me safely back here.

She wondered what time it was, so with some effort, she turned her head towards the clock on the wall and saw that it was twelve minutes past four in the morning. Slowly she sat up on the sofa, even though the urge to lie down again was very strong.

I think I need to drink some water.

With great effort and a few stumbles along the way, Carla arrived at the kitchen sink, poured herself a mug full of water and drank it swiftly down. She returned to the sofa as quick as she could to lie down again, even though her head was still spinning and pounding, she soon fell asleep again.

About an hour later, while in a restless drowsy sleep, she became aware of an unusual sound. She recognised the echo of the steel staircase outside, but it was accompanied by an odd, light-footed scratchy sound. She felt a light breeze across her body and realised that the stable doors were still open, as she listened to this odd sound as it grew closer, as if something was coming up the stairs. Was it a rat? Whatever it was appeared to have come to a stop in the middle of the open doors. Then, the silence was shattered by the ear-piercing sound of a cock bellowing out for all he was worth, "*Cocka-doodle-doo.*"

Carla was so startled that she jumped up immediately. As she stared at the cock, he appeared to be getting ready for his second early morning cry, but before he could do this, Carla grabbed a cushion from the sofa and threw it in his direction. The bird got out of the way just in time and sped off with wings flapping and an assortment of indignant clucks.

Carla stood up, and even though she was still dizzy, it wasn't as bad as before. She walked over to the sink again and had two more mugs of water. As she came to, she looked out of the small window near the sink and saw Henry and Sophie coming out of the farmhouse hand in hand. They turned to each other for a parting kiss, and then Sophie hugged Henry like she hated having to leave his side.

Carla was still struggling to come to terms with being awake, and the rude awakening she had just received. So, she didn't give much thought to the two ill-matched lovers, although under normal circumstances it would have been an intriguing sight to observe. Her only thought now was to get back on the sofa and sleep.

Her sleep was disturbed once more by Marie gently trying to wake her, and saying in a caring tone, "Come on now you big drinker, I've got something to make you feel better."

Marie put her arm behind Carla's shoulder and helped her to sit up.

"That's right, now have some of this, then you will soon feel a lot better."

Marie then held a drinking glass to Carla's mouth and urged her to drink from it. The glass contained a small amount of a dark coloured liquid.

"There you are, good girl, you sleep it off and I'll see you later on."

At nine-thirty Carla woke up, and sat up on the sofa, she was surprised by how much better she now felt. She got to her feet, feeling quite steady, and then she walked out onto the balcony. It was already a bright and sunny day as expected, due to the continuing heatwave. As she looked around her Carla saw the Collie dog, Max, still lazily rooted to the same spot where she saw him yesterday. She heard the other dog, Ginger yapping away somewhere behind the farm buildings and thought, *Well, Ginger's started work this morning even if Max hasn't.*

Then she looked towards the stables, which were a hive of activity as some horses were being saddled up ready for riding.

As she observed, Marie came out of her stable and looked towards *The Old Mill.* She gave a friendly wave, and Carla waved back.

Well, Marie looks a whole lot happier than yesterday when I first saw her at the stables, when she was rocking back and forth to comfort herself.

Carla went back inside to make herself a coffee and have a light breakfast. Still thinking about the improvement in Marie since yesterday, Carla then recalled some of the conversation from the night before about how Marie moved in cycles and how Marie appeared to be improving recently.

Half an hour later, Carla decided to take a walk and explore *Prosperity Farm and Stables* a little. Just as she was descending the outdoor staircase a car pulled up in the yard and an older lady got out of it and said: "I've come for some eggs." A smile formed across her face as she said, "There wasn't any on the roadside stall. Have you seen Henry?"

"No, sorry, I haven't seen him this morning."

"Oh, don't worry. I know my way around. I'll find him somewhere." And with that, she headed towards the farmhouse in search of Henry.

Carla made the short walk to the stables hoping to see Marie. She enjoyed the brightness and warmth of the sun.

It is going to be another hot day again.

When Carla arrived at the stables, she made her way to the stable door that she had seen Marie coming out of earlier. Seeing Marie inside with her back towards her, Carla stood in the doorway and enquired, "You must be Marie?"

Marie turned around and replied, "That's me, Carla. Nice to see you back on your feet again."

Although Marie looked much happier than yesterday, up close there was still no hiding a face full of pain and unhappiness behind the smile.

"I hope you didn't mind me giving you my hangover-cure?"

"No, not at all. I have to admit it appears to have worked wonders for me. I feel like a new person, compared to how I was feeling a few hours back."

"Excellent, I am pleased it worked for you. I knew it would help you. I've never seen it fail. Even so, please don't drive anywhere this morning. My hangover cure only relieves the symptoms. You still have a lot of alcohol in your system, as any policeman with a breathalyser kit would be only too happy to prove to you. You still need to take it easy this morning."

"Sensible words of warning, which I will follow. Thanks again for giving me your hangover cure. I was wondering, what's in it?"

There was a short silence, then Marie said seriously, "Trust me, you don't want to know."

Carla laughed. "I suspect you are right. So long as it works, I don't need to know."

Just then Marie moved aside, allowing Carla to see her extremely well-polished saddle. Carla walked up to it, even in the relatively low light of the stable, it shone magnificently, and Carla could see her reflection in it.

"Oh, wow would you look at that? I can see my face in it."

Carla paused to take it in and then added, "As I understand it there are different types of saddles, would I be right in saying that this is a *General Purpose Saddle.*"

"Oh yes, it is just an ordinary *General Purpose Saddle,*" Marie said proudly.

"Oh, wow! I've never seen anything like it. However, did you get the leather to shine like that?"

"To get it to look like that took me many hours of polishing, and plenty of elbow grease."

For the next few minutes, Marie enthusiastically explained to Carla every minute detail of saddle polishing. When she ran out of things to say there was a brief silence between them, then Marie changed the subject to start the conversation going again.

"Anyway, that is enough from me rabbiting on about saddles."

"Oh, don't worry. It is quite enlightening and the results speak for themselves. It's all very interesting."

"Thank you, even so, moving on, did you see the news last night? The Moonraker Hotel in Bath was the top story with floating boulders in the hotel lobby."

"I did, well actually I was there."

"Really?" Marie said, surprised. "That is interesting, how did you come to be there for the big opening."

"Well, I have a journalist friend and she invited me to tag along with her. It really was quite something to see. They even had a Nikola Tesla lookalike there too, have you heard of him?"

Marie's face dropped upon hearing the name Nikola Tesla. Carla tried to end her fast-moving conversation, "Some of the journalists there were speculating whether it actually was Tesla."

Marie now looked very sad. After a short silence between them, Marie quietly said, "Yes, I know all about Tesla and his work."

"Sorry, it looks like I have somehow said the wrong thing?"

"There is no need to apologize, you wouldn't have known."

Marie drew breath and then continued, "My husband was into free energy and that sort of thing. Oh, he wasn't in the same league as Nikola Tesla by any means, but my husband did have a few successes of his own. My Terry invented, or perhaps discovered might be the more accurate term, I'm not really sure which, because he liked to keep his work fairly secret, as they do. Terry successfully came up with his own free energy device that would save all the worlds' energy problems and set us up for life too. Some pretty big names in the field of energy wanted to buy it from him, and for a huge sum, but they wanted to bury it to protect their own existing interests. Terry, like Tesla, wanted everyone to benefit from his work, and to make the world a better, cleaner, safer place, so he wouldn't sell. Then one day, Terry, just disappeared." Marie sniffed.

"I have unfortunately learnt since his disappearance, that people who find various answers to solving the free energy problem, and yes, there are many, usually meet with an unfortunate end, if they don't keep quiet, or sell when they are asked to."

Carla struggled for a reply, "I'm sorry, I don't know what to say to that Marie, honestly I don't. Other than I feel for you and the unfortunate situation you have found yourself in."

"I know, it sounds like a load of far-fetched conspiracy theory rubbish, doesn't it? My man is missing. I don't know where he is, or what happened to him. Is he alive, or is he dead? I do not know."

"I'm so sorry, Marie."

Silence befell them again.

"It is such a strange thing to have to live with," Marie said, still lost in her thoughts. Trying to take her mind elsewhere and put a brave face on it, Marie said, "Even so, moving on. This heatwave is due to step up even more from today, so they say."

"Yes, that is what they keep telling us. Someone told me last night that there is a lady around here who is convinced that this heatwave is going to end with a big storm."

"Oh yes, that would be Kirra," Marie said with an amused smile across her face. "Kirra is lovely. She is a bright, intelligent lady too, but she is a very unique and singular type of person with her own way of looking at things. Some of her ideas seem a bit strange, but hey, who knows. Maybe she is more enlightened than the rest of us. Kirra believes that this heatwave will end with an enormous storm and out of a clear blue sky too, if you can believe such a thing."

"Well, if it happens, then it will surely be something worth seeing."

"Indeed it will. If you see a lady with a pair of dowsing rods in her hands, then that will be Kirra. She is quite friendly, so introduce yourself, and I am sure she will tell you all about this impending great storm."

"If I see her I might just do that."

"Great, when I think about it, me and Kirra have one thing in common; neither of us owns a horse."

"I suppose that is true, but I hear that you are in the market for one."

"Oh yes, I am. But I don't want just any old nag of a horse. I want a horse that, when I look it in the eye we connect, we understand each other. Many people around here don't get that."

"I understand what you mean. A horse is a very intelligent animal, and certain horses and riders can form a very strong bond."

Marie gave an approving nod, "That's right. I am glad to see that you understand me. I am not in a rush, so I'll keep polishing that saddle until the right horse comes along. I am looking forward to seeing a few people's faces around here when I do finally get my own horse. I suspect that even Henry doesn't believe that I am ever going to buy one. "

"Oh, I am sure you will."

"Talking about Henry," Marie said with a curious look on her face, "What do you make of him?" A smirk gently came across Carla's face, "Well," she paused, "You have got to hand it to Henry he certainly has some rare qualities."

They both now shared a knowing grin, and Carla continued, "I must confess, for an older guy he really has it. That hard to define X factor or charisma."

"Oh yes, he does indeed. Don't you just wish all the men in the world were like him?"

"That would be very nice indeed, but despite Henry being such an amazing guy. I am not looking for romance on my holiday."

"All the ladies say that when they are staying at *The Old Mill,* a few might even truly mean it when they say it, but before their two weeks are up they have fallen into his arms, and of course his bed."

Carla laughed it off saying dismissively, "Oh, I've heard that prediction a few times now, and maybe it becomes a self-fulfilling prophecy."

This led to some amusing light banter between them before Carla finally said, "It has been nice chatting, but I had better let you get back to your polishing."

"Yes indeed, or else I will never get a decent shine on it," Marie joked.

"I was going to buy some eggs from the stall at the farm entrance, but I don't think there are any available at the moment, because a lady pulled into the yard, not that long ago looking for Henry, so she could buy some eggs from him."

Marie burst out laughing, almost as if Carla had said something very naïve.

"What, what did I say?" Carla innocently enquired as Marie laughed even more.

"So, you would like to buy some eggs from Henry, would you?"

"Yes, I would."

Marie laughed again. Carla looked bemused. Clearly, there was more to these eggs. Just then Tracy walked in, "I thought I heard Marie laughing, it has been so long since I heard her laugh, that I thought I had better come and check if she was all right."

Marie was struggling to get her words out through the laughter, but eventually said, "I'm sorry, it is just that Carla wants to buy some eggs from Henry."

Barely had she got those words out, when Tracy fell into fits of laughter, as she caught the moment too.

Carla turned to look at Tracy hoping to gain some understanding as to what was so funny. The laughing stopped and was replaced with a big smirk on Tracy's face.

"If you really don't know, then someone better tell you."

"Yes, I think so," Carla said politely.

"Carla, it is like this. Strangely, I feel almost too embarrassed to tell it, actually," Tracy paused and then continued, "Okay then, so here it is. You must have seen quite a few free-range chickens walking around the place, and as we all know free-range hens lay their eggs all over the place. The thing is, there are never any eggs to sell, or very rarely, despite the stall and sign at the farm entrance."

"Oh yes, I have seen the chickens around the place, I even had a rude awakening by a cock this morning." Upon hearing this line, Marie's laughter was excited again. "So tell me, why aren't there any eggs for sale?"

"That is easy to answer, that lazy dog Max eats them all."

Carla looked at Tracy in puzzlement, "That lazy dog Max, the dog that never moves, eats all the free-range eggs?"

"Yes, that's right. That is the only thing that dog does in a day. Apparently, at some awful time like three or four o'clock in the morning, Max quietly trots around the farm and finds the eggs the hens have laid, and eats them all. The eggshells too, apparently. Then he returns to his favourite spot and does nothing all day."

"So if there are no eggs for sale, and I imagine that there haven't been any eggs for sale in a long time, why then do women turn up here asking Henry if he has any eggs for sale?"

Tracy smiled, "Come on, Carla. Surely, you can figure that one out. To be with Henry, of course. It gives them an excuse to call in and talk to him."

"Talk with him, is that all?"

Tracy smirked, "No, of course that is not all. You know other things happen too."

There was a brief silence as Carla tried to take it all in, and then just as Carla was about to ask another question she heard the sound of a bell rhythmically ringing. At first, she presumed that it was a church bell some distance away, like the one she thought she heard yesterday. Then she looked at Tracy, and Tracy returned the look with a knowing smile.

Just then Fiona walked in and said, "Sounds like another satisfied customer."

The Photo Shoot
Chapter 5

After a very enjoyable chat with Marie, Tracy and Fiona, and a full tour of the stables with them, Carla walked back towards the farmhouse. After hearing about Max's love for free-range eggs, somehow she just felt like meeting him. Max was resting in his usual spot on the front porch, with his head nestled between his two outstretched front legs. As Carla approached him, Max raised his eyes to look at her and he wagged his tail gently.

"Hello Max," said Carla in a warm and gentle voice. "How are you today?"

She knelt and began to gently stroke him. She was surprised by how soft and shiny his coat was.

"Well Max, I have heard that eggs are very good for a dogs coat, maybe there is some truth in that. It sounds like you have a liking for eggs, so maybe you can help to prove this theory."

Max was enjoying all the fuss and attention, but even so he didn't trouble himself with any unnecessary movement. Carla took her hand off him expecting Max to turn towards her or sit upright, but Max didn't move.

"No wonder they have nick-named you lazy dog. You really do not trouble yourself much."

Carla gave him one final stroke on the back, "Well, my friend, if you can't give something back, then that will have to do for you." She got up and returned to *The Old Mill.*

When she was back inside *The Old Mill,* she made herself a mug of coffee and stood in the doorway with her coffee mug and a cookie. As she stood there, she waited for the sound of a bell, *Look at me listening out for the sound of a chiming bell somewhere out there. I don't know why when I don't really believe anything anyone has to say about them so far.*

Carla then went inside and sat on the sofa. While her coffee cooled, she enjoyed the view outside and occasionally glanced over the books on her coffee table. Carla picked up the copy of *Think and Grow Rich,* she opened the first page and read the inscription again.

To Henry. Thanks for everything. Love Judith.

She muttered, "Clearly this is Henry's book. I wonder just what 'everything' might have been." She opened the book where she had left a bookmark inside. "Chapter Two – Desire." Upon reading the word *desire* in a book that clearly belonged to Henry, she couldn't resist a slight chuckle to herself.

"I suspect the word desire and Henry might be a good fit together."

As Carla pondered this, she heard the sound of a small animal running up the steel staircase. Suddenly, Ginger, the Jack Russel Terrier, arrived in the middle of the doorway, looking full of life and energy, with his panting tongue hanging out.

"I wonder what you want." She said as she snapped her cookie in half. "Here you go." She tossed one half of the cookie towards him. With a slight jump, he caught it and quickly devoured it. Then Ginger noticed the other half of the cookie between Carla's fingers and ran through the doorway, jumped over the coffee table and landed directly beside Carla on the sofa.

"I bet you have done that before, haven't you? I should tell you off really for being a naughty dog, but you are so cute."

Carla roughly stroked Ginger in a clawing fashion, which the little dog appeared to revel in, enjoying every moment of it. After some fuss, Carla said fondly, "Oh, you are a lovely little dog, and a lot more sociable than lazy old Max. Do you want the other half of my biscuit?"

Ginger let out a little bark as if to say that he did. Carla gave him the other half and he finished it off quicker than the first.

"Sorry, all gone now, there is no more."

After a minute or two more of rough play and stroking, Ginger jumped off the sofa as if to state that playtime was over. He ambled away under the coffee table and made his way to the doorway again. He glanced back to double-check that there was no more food on offer. He then looked down from the high ground of the balcony as if he was lord and master of all. Something caught his attention, so he barked at it in earnest and then took off running down the stairway in pursuit of his latest quest.

Carla laughed at his little performance and his big attitude, and then picked up her coffee, which was now just the right temperature for drinking. As the first few sips went down, she noticed a subtle pressure in her head easing, which she hadn't been aware of before. This served as a gentle reminder of the drinks from the night before and the fact that there must still be quite a bit of alcohol in her system, which Marie's hangover cure could only relieve the symptoms.

"I think it is time to sit here and read chapter two of *Think and Grow Rich*, while drinking a few coffees, to help put last night behind me."

After drinking three mugs of coffee and reading chapter two of the book, she began to realise how much clearer her mind was becoming.

"Despite Marie's hangover cure, which was a great help it must be said, my mind must have been a bit foggier than I realised this morning," Carla reflected aloud for a moment. "Anyway, it was sort of an accident that I had a bit too much to drink last night, as I didn't set out with the intention of having too much."

Carla waited for some comment from her inner mind, but none came, "And as I know from experience, there are some days that my inner mind never talks to me, hangover days appear to be one of them."

After a light lunch, Carla gathered up a few things in a tote bag to take with her up to the fallen tree in the lane that Henry had recommended to her the previous day. Carla put on her sunglasses and threw her tote bag onto her shoulder, and then she walked out onto the balcony where she found the warmth of the direct sunlight quite striking.

Oh my, I swear it is getting even hotter every day.

As she walked, she momentarily touched the steel handrail, but the heat of the sun had made it too hot to hold on to for long. When she was at the bottom of the staircase she put on a wide brim floppy sun hat, which provided some shade and some much-needed protection from the heat of the sun. She entered the farm lane through the gate near the stables. No sooner had she closed the gate behind her when Ginger appeared through a small hole under the garden hedge. He walked a few strides in

67

front of Carla with his little legs going at a pace as if he seemed to know where she was going as he led the way for her.

Arriving at the fallen tree, lying across the lane near the brow of the hill, she thought, *Oh, this looks like the ideal place to while away a few hours just drawing a little and relaxing a lot, no wonder Henry recommended it. It is a nice spot to lose myself in my thoughts and arrive at a new place in my mind, to help to find a new direction in life.*

Ginger jumped onto the trunk of the tree.

"Oh, so you are going to show me around, are you?"

Ginger trotted along the trunk some way, then he came to a stop, turned around and sat down after letting out a yap.

"Oh, I see. Perfect, just perfect."

Carla could now see that Ginger was trying to show her a perfect sitting position and a makeshift shelf too. Carla recalled Henry saying how the last lady to stay in *The Old Mill* would sit in this old tree for hours with binoculars in her hand and a book on birds from the bookcase. He had said that she loved it up here on this tree.

Carla looked at the tree with a new, keener eye and observed how Henry must have cut off some of the tree branches with a power saw just in front of one particularly large upright branch. This created a wide seating area for several people or a great place for one person to stretch out their legs across the broad horizontal trunk, while resting their back on the broad upright branch behind them.

Ginger jumped onto the makeshift shelf as Carla tried putting her feet up on the trunk with her back resting on the upright branch.

"Oh yes, little dog, this is good, and surprisingly comfortable too."

Then she turned her head a little to her left to inspect the makeshift shelf. "Ginger my little friend, I don't think that I have ever seen half a scaffolding plank put to such good use before."

As she observed the half a scaffolding plank set between two small branches, she noticed a few circular marks on it. "Ginger, if I were *Sherlock Holmes* I would deduce that a man and a woman had been drinking here. She drank white wine, because red wine would have left a red circular mark. And, the evidence from the larger circle would suggest a pint glass; usually the mark of a man's drink. A pint of cider, or scrumpy as some might call it, I suspect. I also surmise from the half scaffolding plank, that this couple had a very small portable barbeque here too. This is quite obvious *Watson*, sorry, I mean Ginger, because why else would a plank of this size be used, and so firmly fitted? And as you may have already noticed, there are slight burn marks from a heat source at one end."

Carla paused, almost as though she was waiting for a comment from Ginger, but obviously, none came.

"And there is one last thing that *Sherlock Holmes* would clearly seduce, I mean deduce, from all this evidence. A good time was had by all."

Ginger let out a little groan as he settled and lay down.

"I thought as much. Case solved."

Carla thought, *you don't need to be Sherlock Holmes to figure out that this is where Henry Farmer appears to have entertained one of his many lovers.* After reflecting on this for a few moments, she emptied the contents of her tote bag across the wooden shelf: binoculars, *Pocket Guide to British Birds*, *Think and Grow Rich*, a large artist's sketchbook, and a large pencil set in a flat wooden box. Ginger lay at one end of the wooden shelf and took no notice of the assorted items Carla had just placed near him.

Carla looked at him and said, "You know what Giger, I could sing to you, I do have a great voice. I was a tribute act singer for a time, but that all came to a crashing end."

Then she said glumly, "All thanks to my so-called journalist friend Lying Lynn."

"Any other day my inner voice would be encouraging me to take singing back up again. Maybe that ship has sailed after all."

Carla took a moment to reflect on this and then she picked up the large sketchbook and used it to fan herself, "Boy it's hot today."

As she fanned herself, she looked at the view around her. The fallen tree was near the top of the sloping green pasture, behind the farmhouse and farm buildings and from this vantage point, Carla had a good overview of the *Prosperity Farm and Stables.* At the centre of the field stood an old wooden barn, quite out of keeping with any other building found on the farm. For an artist, this good-sized barn with its rustic waney-edged boards, set upon each other like rows of a sliced tree, would make an ideal subject for her to draw. Carla looked at it with a keen eye. The barn was a little offset and it did not appear to line up with the farmhouse or any other building on the farm. Two large open wooden doors faced her, but due to the strange offset nature of the barn, she could not see very far inside it. The little that she could see, through the big doors, provided her with a glimpse of a few small rectangular bales of straw.

"Ginger, I think we will have to check that barn out soon. I will probably have a go at drawing it too."

She opened her box of drawing pencils and took out a well-used pencil, a bit shorter than the others in the box, and then she tapped her sketchbook with it and said, "But today Ginger my little friend, I think I will start by drawing you. So please don't move."

Carla began by etching out a very light outline of Ginger's head, and then she added a very faint outline for the ears and his nose. She was beginning to get engrossed in what she was doing when her concentration was broken by the sound of horses approaching. When she looked up, she saw three people she knew coming down the hill, back towards the stables.

Stephany was on the first horse, and when she was very close to Carla's tree she called back to Tracy and Fiona, who were riding behind her, "I told you we would have to watch it with this one. She has only been here a day and already she wants to buy eggs from Henry. Honestly, can you believe some people?" She said dismissively in her usual dry, sarcastic humour before letting out a playful wicked laugh.

Carla laughed it off as Stephany passed by, followed by Tracy who gave Carla a pleasant smile. When Stephany passed by she pretended to fan herself with her hand saying, "Watch out Carla, Kirra thinks there is a storm coming; I hope you don't get too wet."

"Don't worry. I think that I should be okay today," Carla replied as she looked to the sky above.

"Only if you are sure, the storm is coming out of a clear sky, apparently," Fiona added with a chuckle.

71

As Carla watched the three go by, she noticed an open-top Jeep pulling up near the gate entrance to the farm lane. A man got out of it and Henry came to meet him, and they shook hands. A second vehicle pulled up behind the Jeep, and three ladies got out of it.

Carla looked at the binoculars on the shelf and said quietly to herself, "Don't do it, resist the temptation to be a nosy-parker." She stared at the binoculars for a while longer and then picked them up and pointed them in the direction of the farm. As she focused the binoculars, the man now talking to Henry came into view. Around his neck, he had a camera with a large lens, and somehow he just had the general appearance of a professional photographer. Carla took a closer look at the three ladies who had just arrived. Although they were all very casually dressed, their hair, makeup, and general persona indicated that they were all professional models; all of them in their early twenties. Carla lowered her binoculars and said to herself, "Look at me, I must not do things like that. Note to self, binoculars are just for bird watching."

Carla was a bit curious as to why there would be a photographer and three models at the farm, so she raised the binoculars again to take another look, then she noticed one of the models was very taken with Henry.

"Oh please, I am the only female around here who makes an effort to resist this man's many charms."

As she watched, the photographer introduced Henry to each model in turn, and polite pleasantries appeared to be exchanged between them. When Henry was introduced to the model that clearly fancied him, she looked slightly awkward and embarrassed because she couldn't hide the effect he had on her.

Carla put the binoculars back on the shelf and said to Ginger, "I'm sure that you have seen it all before, haven't you Ginger?"

Carla went back to sketching Ginger. A few minutes later, she raised her head again and looked down the lane to see Henry and the photographer followed by the three models that were now all walking up the lane and heading towards the old wooden barn. Carla noticed the model that appeared to fancy Henry was falling behind everyone else and she was taking her wristwatch off. After discreetly putting it into her bag, she ran to catch up with the others and wasted no time in starting a conversation with Henry. Carla shook her head and returned to sketching Ginger. Occasionally, she lifted her head and looked towards the barn, which was just about close enough to see people without the aid of binoculars. Henry was watching with interest as the photographer took photos of his three models in various poses in front of the barn doors. After taking enough outdoor photos, Carla observed the photographer gesturing to the group to go inside the old timber barn. Strangely, Henry appeared a little embarrassed and was making excuses to leave, but the models appeared to be encouraging him to join them inside. Eventually, Henry left and the photographer and his three models went inside and out of sight. Carla looked at Ginger and said, "You are an excellent little subject to draw, nothing distracts you, unlike the artist drawing you. I really wonder why they wanted Henry in the barn with them, and why he did not want to join them. It is probably best that I don't know, if you ask me."

About an hour later Carla finished her drawing of Ginger, "There you are, little fellow," she said proudly showing the drawing to Ginger, "And not a bad likeness of you either. I can't believe that you actually sat still that long, you know what they say about working with children and animals. You deserve a treat for that, don't you?"

She put her hand inside the tote bag and pulled out a packet of biscuits, "I have been keeping these out of the sunlight, and my bottle of water too."

Ginger sat up quite excited. He knew a packet of biscuits when he saw one. Carla opened them and gave him the first one from the pack while making a fuss of him. After that, he stood up and jumped off the wooden shelf and trotted off, looking all pleased with himself.

"That must mean that you are all done for the day, I assume," she joked.

Carla then took her bottle of water out of the tote bag and opened it.

"Boy, it is hot today."

She drank down plenty of water and looked back towards the wooden barn in the middle of the field, just as the photographer and his three models were coming out.

"They look hot too."

She watched them as they walked back towards the farm lane and through the gate near their vehicles. Carla spent a few minutes with the binoculars trying to follow a number of birds in flight, before finally explaining to herself, "Would you birds mind flying still for a moment, I can't follow you if you keep moving around."

She sighed and then added, "I don't think that I am doing this right somehow, but at least I can try again tomorrow."

The sound of car engines starting drew her attention back in the direction of the farm. Soon the photographer and his models were driving down the driveway as Carla pondered their photoshoot and the choice of location.

Just then, her phone rang. Picking it up, she smiled upon seeing the name on the screen, Lying Lynn.

Without stopping to say hello Lynn went straight into an agitated rant, "Would you ever believe it? I mean ever believe it! It is as if she somehow knew that I was on to her. First, she sneaks into the film location and her makeup trailer unseen. I know she was there. Somehow she sneaked passed me totally unseen, and believe me, I miss nothing when I set my mind on a thing. No one anywhere near the film set, I mean no one, will talk to me. And twice, two huge security guys have forcibly removed me. How can something like this be happening to me?"

Carla tried not to laugh, and then tried to sound supportive, "Oh Lynn, I am sorry to hear that."

Without listening Lynn continued in a more calculating tone, "If she thinks that she can beat me, then she has another thing coming. I will get the dirty low down on her in the end."

Carla winced upon hearing words of ill will towards Sophie Archer.

"No one has the upper hand over me for long."

Then she said more calmly, "Despite all the setbacks of the day, I have managed to find out one thing, though. She will be in her little red car in half an hour, and then she will be travelling to see her new and very newsworthy lover. I am sitting in my car right now, four cars away from hers." In a very mean voice, she said, "I've got her now, oh the sweet smell of success."

"Perhaps you should leave her alone Lynn, go back to the Moonraker Hotel and find out more about the floating stones. Maybe that is the better story in the end."

Angrily Lynn retorted, "Floating stones. Oh, who cares about them flaming floating stones, it is Sophie's head I want, served up to the media, and all thanks to me."

Carla was quite horrified at Lynn's determined and vexed attitude towards Sophie Archer. She needed an excuse to end the call quickly and let Henry know in good time to warn her.

"Sorry Lynn, the signal is weak here, I think I am losing you, hello, hello."

She pressed the end call button and rolled through the contact list on her phone to find Henry's mobile phone number. "I know I put it in here somewhere when I booked the holiday, oh here it is under, *The Old Mill*."

After finding it, she rang it straight away to let Henry know, he thanked her and then ended the call quickly so that he could call Sophie immediately to warn her.

Carla decided to sit in the tree a bit longer and read the next chapter of *Think and Grow Rich* – "Faith." After reading it with some interest, she closed her eyes and relaxed as she thought about the chapter she had just read and how it related to her own life. After some time Carla opened her eyes again, packed everything back into her tote bag and started walking back to *The Old Mill*. When she arrived back in the yard, she saw Henry approaching. As he walked towards her, she couldn't stop herself from thinking, *you really are in every way, one gorgeous guy.*

He looked very pleased to see her. "Thank you so much for the tip-off. That was a close call for Sophie. I asked her if it was best if she stayed away from here tonight, but she insists on coming over to see me. Apparently, the film company has a wide assortment of vehicles that she can borrow, so she will be able to quietly slip away in one unnoticed."

"That has all worked out well then. I am so pleased that Sophie has been saved from the cruel attentions of the media. I wish her well, I truly do."

"I must say, without your help, Sophie would be in a right pickle now."

Henry noticed a small car coming down the driveway, "Who is that coming down the drive now, I don't recognise the car."

"Maybe it is Sophie?"

"I don't think so, I would have thought from what she told me earlier that it will be at least another hour before she gets here."

The little car pulled up in the yard and Carla recognised its driver straight away. It was the photographic model from earlier that afternoon. Carla recalled how she had trouble trying to hide the fact that she fancied Henry. She also remembered her taking her watch off and putting it in her bag for some reason. The young lady got out of her car, and Carla said to Henry with a slight smirk on her face, "I believe it's you she wants, so I will leave you to it."

Henry smiled, "I believe that you are right."

Carla walked away and gave the young model a pleasant smile as they passed each other. As Carla walked towards the steel staircase, she overheard the model say to Henry in a slow, subtle seductive tone, "I appear to have lost my wristwatch earlier today in that old wooden barn of yours. I don't want to go there on my own, could you come with me to help me look for it, please?"

Realising the game the model was playing, Carla smiled privately to herself and began walking up the steel staircase, her echoing footsteps now preventing her from overhearing any more of their conversation.

As she reached the open doors of *The Old Mill,* Carla noticed Henry and the model walking towards the gate to the lane.

I bet she must have that wristwatch in her bag anyway, but I doubt that is what she is truly looking for, she thought to herself.

Carla took a cold shower to help cool off before settling down on the sofa with a cool drink to read another chapter of *Think and Grow Rich.* About an hour later, Carla heard another vehicle coming down the long drive. She stood up and stretched a little before walking out onto the balcony. "It is going to be a lovely evening, and a hot one," she mumbled. A small dark-coloured van passed by her and pulled up in the yard. The young model's car was gone. "I hope she found what she was looking for."

The door of the small van opened and Sophie Archer got out of it looking like a million dollars in a long red dress.

Spotting Carla, she enquired, "Are you, Carla?" She nodded, as Sophie came closer.

"Thank you so much. I can't tell you how much I appreciate what you have done for me."

"That is no problem at all. I love your films by the way."

"Thanks, if you want, you and I can have a good chat sometime soon, and I will tell you all about my latest film. But for now, I had better go inside and keep out of sight in case your journalist friend has found out where I am. Thanks again."

Carla went back inside and sat on the sofa. Just as she picked up her book again, a text message came through from

Lynn. Carla laughed as she read, *I am still waiting for Sophie, they must still be filming, but she will not escape me. I will wait here all night if I have to.*

Henry's New Tractor
Chapter 6

The next morning Carla was lying asleep naked on the sofa with the front stable doors and the rear bedroom window open to let the breeze through. She had read over half of *Think and Grow Rich* before she tried to go to sleep in the rear bedroom, wearing a light nightdress, but the night had been so hot that she took it off; an hour or so after that, she left the bedroom to sleep on the sofa, because it was a much cooler there. It was now five in the morning and everything was quiet and still and Carla was deep asleep. Just then, the silence was broken by the ear-piercing sound of a cock bellowing out for all he was worth "*Cocka-doodle-doo.*"

Carla slowly sat up and came to. When she opened her eyes she saw the cock strutting away.

"They never mentioned you in the brochure," Carla complained as she listened to his faint echo on the steel staircase outside as he made his way back to the yard, where he rang out another "*Cocka-doodle-doo,*" just before Ginger chased him off with a few barks.

Carla opened a small bottle of water she had left on the coffee table the night before and drank it all down. She heard the faint sound of a chiming bell.

"It is five in the morning, whatever is causing that bell to ring right now, I don't want to know about it."

After that, she lay back down on the sofa and went back to sleep. Around six, she woke again when she heard the voices of Henry and Sophie outside, saying their early morning goodbyes to each other in the yard. She sat up on the sofa again, as she listened to the somewhat surreal sound of a film star driving away in a little van.

Quietly she said, "Well, that is not something you experience every day."

Carla's inner voice commented, *Come on Carla, Henry is in the yard right now, why don't you take your naked little self onto the balcony and show Henry what you have to offer him; you know you want to, deep down.*

"Oh, so you are back again, are you? And I don't want to offer Henry anything at all. Thank you, as you well know." She paused, and then added, "Day off yesterday was it?"

As you know there are a few days that I never talk to you at all, and days, when you are worse after drink are one of them, as is any other time when your mind is foggy or messed up.

"Well, it made a nice change not having you going on at me."

I never go on at you. Please think of me more as your inner guide or spiritual adviser, most other people would.

"Whatever, but please don't keep telling me to take up singing again."

I haven't mentioned that for a while. But since you have brought up the subject, I think you should take it up again, that is where your true gift and passion is to be found. Ignore the hurtful things that so-called friend Lying Lynn said about your voice, and cross her off your list of friends. You are better off without her, anyway.

81

"If Lying Lynn finds out that I have been tipping off Sophie Archer, she will not be my friend for much longer anyway."

I know you think that she is a useful person to have around. Compared to the so-called yes men of this world, you do at least get an honest opinion from her, but remember it is only her opinion and not necessarily true.

"Okay. Well, you have a point there. I will think about it some more. I sense that there is something else you want to say to me."

I see, you are getting to know me after all. We truly are a perfect team, you and I. I wanted to say to you that reading, Think and Grow Rich, is the very best thing that you can do right now. So get some clothes on and get on with reading it, and after reading it once, read it again many more times in the years to come. It will be helpful to you in life, in so many ways.

"Why should I read it? I thought it was one of the main tasks of an inner voice to point a person in the right direction in life?"

And indeed it is, and that is what I am doing right now. Please remember, I can only point and advise you, you must do the actual work yourself, which on this occasion means some reading.

Carla paused to think for a moment, but her inner voice interrupted her, *I can hear you, you know. Questioning yourself as to whether an inner voice is a sane thing or not. Let me tell you that everyone has one, believe it or not. While it is sadly true that some inner voices are unhelpful, or just occasionally outright dangerous, in truth, that has more to do with a lack of inner voice training. On the whole, an inner voice is a good thing and well worth cultivating and taking the time to build a strong relationship with.*

"Whatever, it is a bit early in the morning for such a deep intellectual conversation with you?"

It is indeed, but you missed a day yesterday thanks to all that drinking the night before. So, into the shower with you, get dressed and get reading.

At around ten o'clock, Carla finished reading the final chapter of *Think and Grow Rich,* and then she walked out onto the balcony still holding the book in her hand and felt pleased with herself for reading it all. After soaking up some sun, she returned to the relatively cool shade offered by *The Old Mill* and sat on the sofa again.

"I didn't want to be seen standing on the balcony talking to myself."

Of course not, her inner voice said, *but you do feel better for having read the entire book for the first time?*

"Yes, I suppose I do, but I am not sure why you are so certain that I need to read it so many times over. Surely, if I read it once or twice, then I have got the basics, haven't I?"

You certainly have the basics and nothing more.

"But..."

No buts at all, her inner voice stated without hesitation, *trust me, some things you will discover for yourself over time, so read this book often. That is the best advice you will ever receive.*

Carla knew from experience that her inner voice had made its final point and brought this particular subject of conversation to a close for the present moment.

"I assume that the rest of the day is now all my own?" She waited to see if any comment came from her inner voice, but none came.

"Great! Now that is settled. I can grab my drawing stuff and head back to the tree again."

Although excited by this choice, somehow she felt the need to pause and search her feelings. After some thought, Carla decided to take a walk around the farm buildings first, and go back up to the tree in the afternoon. She was not sure why, but this plan felt like a better idea to her.

She put a few broken biscuits into a small bag and put them in her pocket, in readiness for Ginger if she met him. Then she walked onto the balcony and down the stairs. She remembered how Henry had said that she could go anywhere on the farm that she wanted, so she headed towards a ramshackle collection of traditional farm buildings first.

Carla enjoyed exploring all the various farm buildings of differing sizes with many different purposes, both past and present; such as the old, pig sheds, and cow sheds, now mostly used to keep a few hens in.

"So, I bet lazy old Max finds a lot of his eggs around here in the early hours of the morning."

Next, she walked around two large hay barns, which were almost empty at this time of year, but they were presently used mostly to store agricultural machinery in. She heard the sound of hammering from a very large modern building, with a wide tall main doorway.

There was a small side door, which was open so Carla headed towards it. Entering the building, she realised it was the farm's workshop and the place that stored the biggest machinery on the farm. Directly in front of her was a brand new combine harvester. She walked to the front of the machine. From there she looked up at the huge machine with its gleaming paintwork and state of the art technology inside the cab. She stood there for some moments, taking in every detail. Then she heard the hammering sound again and walked around the combine harvester a little more, where she found a very big, brand new four-wheel-drive, Massey Ferguson tractor. She stood in front of that too, and looked at it closely. It had beautiful bright red and silver paintwork. Looking through the cab window, she saw that

84

the seat and all of the controls still had clear plastic covers wrapped over them, which indicated to her that this tractor had not been used yet. She heard the hammering sound again, which appeared to be coming from the rear end of the tractor. When she walked to the back of the tractor she found Henry gently hammering on a small part on the back end of the tractor.

She felt a slight flutter in her chest upon seeing him, and couldn't resist thinking, *he just looks so damn attractive in whatever setting I see him in.*

She spoke to get his attention and wanting to observe his reaction, "I was surprised to hear hammering, it is usually only bells I hear around the place, and even then I am still not quite sure why that is."

Henry raised his head to see her, and a mischievous smile momentarily flashed across his face, upon hearing Carla mention bells.

"Good morning, Carla. Nice to see you."

He carried on hammering a few more times before saying in a satisfied voice, "There that does it. You see Carla, with a brand new machine like this, sometimes things are a bit too tight at first, until the machine has done a bit of work, due to the way all of the components are machined with such precision nowadays, and then covered in layers of bright shiny new paint too. But enough of all that, how are you today?"

"I am fine, thanks, Henry. My dad's old tractor was so old and worn that there was no danger of anything being tight." They both laughed. "I have been walking around your various farm building this morning, and I have ended up here. I can see now where Max must be getting all his eggs from."

"Oh, you have heard about him and what he gets up to in the early hours."

"Oh, yes."

"It is strange, as a farmer throughout the year I am often out and about at all hours, day and night, but as yet I have actually never caught him doing it."

Then he said comically, "Whenever I see Max he is on my front porch. The lazy bloody animal."

Carla laughed, "That sounds like a good description of him." She remembered the model from yesterday and asked, "Did you and that young model find her wristwatch yesterday?"

"Would you believe it? The watch was in her bag the whole time."

Carla observed a bit of a twinkle in his eye as he spoke.

Playing along with it Carla added, "Well, imagine that."
Carla then turned to look at Henry's new tractor.

"I must say, your new tractor and combine harvester look quite impressive. They really do."

"Thank you, I am really looking forward to using them soon for the first time. The combine harvester arrived here late last year, well after the corn-cutting season, but it is all set up now and ready to go for this new season. And my new Massey Ferguson tractor was only just delivered a few weeks back. The guy that brought it here on the back of his lorry was trying to tell me some story about two Jaguar convertibles, a red one and a green one overtaking him on the way here, some kind of race or something. I must confess that I wasn't a good listener when he dropped the new tractor off. I only had eyes and ears for my new Massey Ferguson tractor. You know, boys and their toys and all that."

"Oh yes, I can imagine."

"Have you got any other tractors around here?"

"Yes, an old blue one, a Ford 4000, actually. It is quite small by modern standards. Most of the time I just leave it hooked up to an equally old farm trailer with odds and ends for fencing and hedge repairs on it. I will be getting it out later on today because I am going to put a post and wire fence in at the top of that sloping field. My old Ford 4000 is no good when it rains though because it does not have a cab. But with this heatwave, I don't think I need to worry about a cab too much at the moment."

"So, what will be the first job for this new tractor of yours?"

"Ploughing will be the first main task for it, but I may well use it for a few smaller jobs here and there before that. I bought a nice new four-furrow plough last year too, so I am well set up now."

"Excellent, how many acres will you be ploughing this year?"

"Ten acres."

Carla laughed, "Yes, of course, you must need all this new machinery for ten acres."

Henry repeated, "Ten acres."

Carla looked a little puzzled, "Why only ten acres?

"Because that is all I need. If I plant and harvest ten acres of corn that will fill my big grain trailer, which is enough corn to feed my chickens all year long. Chickens lay eggs, and I sell the eggs."

Carla now looked even more puzzled and enquired, "But I thought all of the eggs were eaten by Max each day, so there are never any eggs to sell."

"That is very true, unfortunately. I never have any eggs to sell. That lazy dog Max eats them all or at least every egg he can find."

"In business plan terms, that is not a good formula for success is it?"

"No, it is not really," Henry agreed.

"Forgive me asking, but what size is this farm?"

"This farm is around thirty-five acres or just over fourteen hectares using the modern measurement system."

"Forgive me asking, and please feel free to tell me to mind my own business if you want to. After all, you don't have to tell me anything if you don't want to, but my curiosity is quite aroused now. I remember when my late dad had his farm how hard it was to make ends meet, let alone make a profit. Even with any profits from your stables, I cannot quite grasp how you can buy a brand new combine harvester, a brand new big tractor too, to plant ten acres of corn, to feed to chickens whose eggs you never get to sell. Sorry, that does not make any sense to me at all." Then with a genuine smile, she added, "However, if you can make all that work for you and earn some profit too, then I am very pleased for you. Honest, I am."

Henry smiled for a moment. Carla noticed how his smile was very much like the smile of a person whose guilty secret had just been found out. Yet, somehow he controlled it like a person who knew how to show the world only the side of him he wanted to show. Henry moved in a little closer and quietly said in that warm, friendly way of his, "Who said that the purpose of this farm is to make a profit?" He paused before continuing, "You are right, I don't have to tell you anything. However, you are a clever girl, I could see that quality in you from the first moment we met, and I know from what you said to me on your first day here, that you are trying to find a new direction in life. Possibly, you would like to reinvent or rediscover yourself too. So instead of answering your question directly, and because I do like you and wish you well in everything that you do, I will share some wisdom with you instead, because doing that will serve you much better in the long run, if you will think upon it from time to time."

Carla found Henry's vocal tones delicious and they were now directed at her personally, combined with being physically close to him more than ever before. He sent tingles down her spine with every word he spoke.

"Do you know which animal here at *Prosperity Farm and Stables* is, in my opinion, the cleverest animal?" Carla shook her head. Henry continued, "Max, that dog everyone calls lazy. And he is to be sure, especially when you compare him to Ginger, who never stops working away all day long. Personally, I have to say that I dislike laziness in any form, but Max is also very clever and I respect him for that. At some point, Max decided how he wanted to live his life, and he does indeed live his life on his terms. How many people do you know who are living life on their terms? Totally, on their terms?"

"Not one, I know that for sure because strangely enough, I have been thinking about things like that in recent weeks."

"Carla, I once read a book called *Think and Grow Rich*, by *Napoleon Hill*, in fact, I have read it many times over and even now have several copies of that great book. I will spare you the details, but it is enough to say in all honesty, that book changed my life forever, and I have never looked back since discovering it."

"I know that you have read it, because one of your copies is in *The Old Mill* bookcase. I have been reading it myself." Carla added, "The copy with the inscription inside the first page, *To Henry. Thanks for everything, Love Judith."*

"Oh yes, lovely Judith. I remember her well."

He said contently, "Well, if you have read that book then you will have come across a poem inside it called *I bargained with life for a penny."*

Carla nodded. She was surprised by how much his attention was beginning to make her feel weak and helpless around him.

"I used to go through life creating and fighting one disaster after another. I couldn't see that all of the problems in my life, were in truth all of my own making. That poem really made me think about who I was and the choices that I had made."

Henry recited every line of the poem from memory, somehow bringing every word of it to life with perfect diction, feeling, and interpretation.

> *I bargained with life for a penny,*
> *And life would pay no more,*
> *However, I begged at evening*
> *When I counted my scanty store.*

> *For life is a just employer,*
> *He gives you what you ask,*
> *But once you have set the wages,*
> *Why, you must bear the task.*

> *I worked for a menials hire,*
> *Only to learn, dismayed,*

That any wage I had asked of life'
Life would have willingly paid.

(Authors note – Napoleon Hill did not credit the author of the poem in his book, I believe it to be, Jessie B Rittenhouse)

After reciting the poem, Henry paused for a few moments and then said, "Carla, that poem contains so much wisdom, and the book even more so."

Carla reflected for a moment, "Thanks for that Henry, you have brought that poem to life for me in a new way."

Henry stepped back, "No problem, I truly hope it turns out to be of help to you. Anyway, that is enough from me. I had better let you go. You are on holiday after all."

"And you are busy too, so I shouldn't keep you from your work any longer."

As Carla made her way back to *The Old Mill,* she couldn't stop herself from going over in her mind every detail of the conversation she had just had with Henry. She slightly regretted asking Henry some of the more direct questions about his business, yet his answers were intriguing.

Finally, after much thought she began to speculate - *Is that what you are doing Henry Farmer, living life on your terms, but like Max not in a conventional way. Have you applied Napoleon Hill's many excellent success principles from Think and Grow Rich, firstly to make enough money to live life on your financially free terms, and then secondly have you found a way to apply them equally as well, to attract the opposite sex into your life too?*

Kirra

Chapter 7

Carla collected the things she wanted to take with her to the fallen tree and put them in her tote bag. For a moment she considered wearing a dress, but decided that the jeans she already had on were better suited for sitting in a tree.

Just then, a text message from Lynn came through on her phone. *Yesterday = one crap day. Having a quiet morning in the Moonraker watching the floating stones, trying to figure out what has gone wrong?* ☹☹

Carla felt a little sorry for Lying Lynn, but somehow it didn't feel it was quite right to call her at the moment, so she decided to call her later on in the day.

After a light lunch, Carla threw the tote bag on her shoulder and put her sunglasses on. Stepping onto the balcony, the intense heat of the sun prompted her to toss her wide brim floppy sun hat onto her head immediately.

"Surely it cannot get any hotter." Glancing at the steel handrail, she added, "and I am not going to touch that today. No way."

Carla walked down the outdoor staircase and across the yard to the wooden gate leading to the farm lane. As she began walking up the lane she heard Ginger yapping away at something in the old waney-edge wooden barn in the middle of the field and thought to herself, *Well, I hadn't thought of checking out that barn.*

As she approached the barn, Ginger came running out to greet her. Carla made a fuss of him as he lay down on the ground and gave him a few broken biscuits that she had put in her pocket earlier that morning. After a few minutes of fuss, Ginger suddenly sat bolt upright and looked intently towards the farmhouse garden, then he sped off running at full pelt towards a small hole in the garden hedge, which he entered without slowing down at all, yapping all the way.

Carla giggled at his little performance.

"Oh, you silly little dog, but you are just lovely, though." She turned and continued walking the remaining short distance towards the old barn. When she arrived at the old timber barn, she heard an unfamiliar engine sound and looked back towards the gate at the bottom of the lane, where she saw Henry coming through the gate on his old blue Ford 4000 tractor with its trailer in tow.

Not being in any rush, Carla sat down on the grass and watched Henry drive his old Ford tractor up the lane, past the fallen tree, and then up to the top of the sloping field. From there he turned right and travelled along the top of the brow of the hill to the far side of the field. Once there, Henry got off his tractor and grabbed an armful of wooden fencing posts from the back of the trailer. He then walked a short distance along the brow of the hill, with the first six posts for his new fence, placing them at approximately equal distances apart. Then he went back to the trailer, collected a sledgehammer and then returned to the first fencing post he had placed on the ground. He stood the post upright and began to hammer it into the ground.

"Oh my, oh my, why is he doing that kind of work on such a hot day?"

Come on Carla you can't just sit there watching Henry all day, her inner voice commented.

"No you are right about that, but I would like to, though."

She stood up and walked into the barn, through the two wide-open entrance doors at the front end of it. It took a few moments for her eyes to adjust from the strong sunlight outside to the shade of the barn. When able to look about her more clearly, she found the first half of the barn to be almost empty, apart from a small number of small straw bales alongside each wall and several more randomly placed in the centre; which Carla assumed the three models must have used the day before.

Thinking that the randomly placed straw bales made the place look untidy, she dragged them to the side of the barn and placed them neatly along the wall. The rear half of the barn was about half full of neatly stacked small straw bales. Carla walked towards the back of the barn where she found a big heap of loose straw lying in front of the stacked bales. Upon closer inspection, she noticed that the loose straw looked as if two people may have been laying on it together, and commented, "I wonder if that was where Henry was helping that young model to look for her wristwatch?"

For the next few minutes, Carla took a good look around the old wooden barn, before finally deciding to sit in the sunshine on one of the straw bales nearest the entrance. From there she could see the fallen tree, but she soon closed her eyes to relax in the sun and listen to the distant sound of Henry hammering in wooden fencing posts.

Within a few minutes of sitting in the sun, she was becoming very relaxed and gently beginning to drift off, when a woman's voice said cheerfully, "Hello Carla."

Carla opened her eyes to find an older woman dragging a straw bale from the other side of the barn so she could use it to sit opposite Carla, but unlike Carla, she kept her straw bale in the shade. "Oh, it's too hot for me to sit in the heat of the sun for long."

"How do you know my name?"

"Oh, that is easy Carla, everyone around here knows each other and who is staying at *The Old Mill*. So, come on tell me my name, I bet you can quite easily."

Initially, Carla thought that was a strange request, how could she possibly know who this woman was? Looking her over, she spotted two metal rods in her hand,

"Oh yes, an easy enough question to answer. You must be Kirra."

"Yes, that's right, Carla. What was it that gave me away? Was it me being a bit plumpy, my wild looking curly grey hair, a general eccentric look about me, or just my divining rods?"

"Your divining rods, for me that was a total give away."

"So, how are you enjoying yourself here on holiday?"

"I am having a great time so far. Nice quiet days with time for reading, drawing, and the occasional chance to get lost in my own thoughts for a while. Time to think and reflect and all that."

"Sounds good to me. There is too much life in the fast lane these days. No time to rest or think."

"I totally agree with you there," Carla said, nodding in agreement.

"I hear that you have quite a liking for Henry's homemade cider and that other strange drink of his, *Red Tractor Diesel*."

"Oh, you heard about that one, did you?"

"Oh, yes," she said with a hearty chuckle.

"How long have you known Henry?"

"I knew Henry at high school actually, although he can't remember me from back then. I am not surprised really, because I was in the first year of high school, and he was in the final year. Even then, he was surrounded by adoring females. Every girl in school wanted to be his girl. Even though, and quite surprisingly, he was a bit shy back then, but those girls helped him overcome all that." Kirra chuckled.

"Why does it not surprise me that every girl in school wanted to be his girlfriend? I assume he was quite handsome at school."

"Oh yes, he was drop dead gorgeous. Some people are blessed with rare natural talents that the rest of us can never hope to possess, and his rare natural talent is to own a certain attractiveness that we ladies can't fail to appreciate to the full. He has not lost that quality over time. In fact, somehow I think that he has even improved upon it. Enhanced it, might even be a better choice of words. I have never met a man so powerfully, magically, attractive, to a woman."

"Me neither, I must admit it. He certainly has got something special about him, especially for an older guy."

"You may have noticed how he never looks tired either, regardless of how many ladies he has shall we say, entertained that day. That is not a natural talent, and he has somehow mastered that particular area of specialist knowledge."

"I had wondered about that. He does appear to have a lot of stamina." Carla paused and then added, "Interesting, to hear you used the term specialist-knowledge. I have been reading one of Henry's old books from the bookcase in *The Old Mill,* and chapter four is all about *Specialist Knowledge.*"

"Maybe he learnt a lot from that chapter and applied it to *Prosperity Farm and Stables,*" she said with a laugh. "I would also say that on the surface of things he never appears to try too hard at attracting and seducing, but ultimately, even being irresistibly attractive will only get you so far. Creating opportunities to spend time with an assortment of females must be an important element too. I am certain that he must have put in quite a bit of work beforehand to allow things to easily work out in his favour."

Carla began to curiously ask, "Have you ever?" Kirra interrupted

"Oh no, my dear. Henry and I are just two good old mates. We have been friends for a very long time now. It is so odd how our paths have kept crossing over the years. Anyway, I am probably a bit too quirky for him. As a result of all that, we are the only two people around here who have not done that particular time honoured physical act together." She laughed.

"That is not true, because I haven't either."

"Oh, but you will my dear. I can promise you that. Many have told me that once they found themselves in his arms, they just melted like butter. I have never seen a single female staying at *The Old Mill* on holiday deny herself that particular pleasure."

"I am planning to be the first," she said with a laugh.

"Oh yes, my dear, but ask yourself is that particular world record really worth holding?" She laughed.

"Maybe not, but who knows," Carla said with a chuckle. "Moving on to other subjects, I understand that you are quite good with those divining rods in your hand."

"I don't know if I am quite good with them or not really, but I find them quite fascinating to use and I have learnt so much from using them," she said as she waved them around. "This farm does have quite a fascinating energy about it, which is why I love coming here so much with my rods I suppose. I told Henry this place had special energy when he bought it, although he claims not to remember me saying so now. Well, one thing is clear, he has certainly done well for himself here. And he has made himself a lot of money too on the quiet, clever old Henry. He is no fool. That is for certain. He is set up for life now."

"Yes, he does appear to be on top of things, even with Max eating all the free-range eggs he can find."

"You know Carla; nowadays this place is just Henry's playground."

Carla pondered that for a moment and then curiously asked, "Does the term playground extend to his interest in the opposite sex too?"

"I'm afraid so, but I think it is fair to say that he does it so well. Somehow everyone wins and walks away happy in the end."

Carla looked a little hesitant and then asked, "Please forgive me for asking, but what are the bells all about?

"Ah yes, the bells. You noticed them."

"You can't miss them, going off at random times day and night. I am not sure whether to believe what the other girls around here say about them or not. I have also noticed how they begin so rhythmically, but the rhythm falls apart at the finish."

"Carla, say it out loud what do you think the chiming bells are all about?" Kirra said with an amused knowing smile.

"Well," Carla began full of awkwardness, "Actually, there is one thing I want to mention first. I was brought up on a farm, so I know from my own experience just how sound gets, well sort of, bounced off walls, tall sheds and buildings, making its source hard to trace sometimes. Even so, after hearing the chiming bells on a number of occasions now and from different parts of this farm, clearly, the sound is coming from the farmhouse. I think that I am right in saying that there are three different bells too, and each bell has its own distinct ring."

"So far so good, so tell me what is the final missing piece of the jigsaw?"

Carla laughed with a slight sigh, "Well, if I had to make a wild guess, I would say there are three beds, and each bed is on a different floor of the farmhouse. There is a bell attached to each bed and when two people become active enough together the bell chimes." Carla paused, "Am I even close."

"You are pretty much there. Although I have been told each of those bedrooms also contains many other interesting features too, I have no idea what and I am not even sure if I want to know either." She laughed.

"The higher the floor each bedroom is on, the more entertaining the room. Henry has created a sort of contest or rivalry amongst all those he entertains up there in his house. They only make their way slowly up the floors, one bedroom at a time."

Carla looked aghast, "But that is ridiculous, why would anyone even want a bell ringing under their bed at such a private moment?"

Kirra shrugged, "Personally, I would agree with you on that one. But as you know, there appears to be no shortage of takers. There is a bell ringing at least once, most days. Also, as you must have seen there is many a housewife popping in to enquire if there are any eggs for sale."

Carla chuckled, "Oh yes, I have noticed that a few times now, and at all hours of the day."

Carla laughed out loud and said, "Look at us, I hardly know you, and yet look how much ground we have covered in our conversation in the past few minutes."

"We have indeed. I must be having one of my less quirky days. Most of the time people struggle to understand me and any point I am trying to reach when I talk."

"Rest assured, I can grasp everything you are saying."

"Excellent. Now Carla, if you don't mind, I would like to try a reading with you using my rods, if you are okay with that, but if this does not feel right for you then please say so and stop me."

"No, it's fine with me. It should be interesting."

Kirra placed one divining rod in each hand and closed her eyes and tilted her head back a little. Carla watched as the divining rods gently swayed back and forth for almost a minute, before finally coming to rest, pointing in Carla's direction. Kirra made a gentle humming sound, which went on for some time, then Kirra began to speak slowly with her eyes still closed. "You have a friend. You don't like her much. Do not trust her. She has hurt you in the past, and she will continue to bring you pain and trouble. You must get her out of your life as soon as you can."

The humming returned for about half a minute then Kirra spoke again, "I sense that you feel that you have lost your way in life a bit," there was a short pause then Kirra continued, "You have not really lost your way, but you have allowed others to hold you back from doing what you love the most. Your future is in your hands, but you must stand up for yourself more and ignore the opinions of others."

Again, Kirra was silent for some time before slowly speaking again, "I see a book. You have been reading a book. This book will be very useful to you. This book has a special power and energy all of its own, which forms a link with the reader if they are open to it. You must keep reading it over time."

Slowly Kirra lowered her hands and the divining rods fell forward. She opened her eyes, but now she looked physically drained of energy. Looking ahead, she said weakly, "Oh, that does take a lot out of me. I rarely used my rods that way because it drains me so. I just somehow sensed from talking to you that you needed it. I hope it was helpful to you."

Kirra turned to look at Carla and gave her a comforting smile, when she saw tears forming in Carla's eyes.

Struggling to speak a little Carla said, "Yes, I think that was very helpful. Thank you, I needed to hear all that."

She rubbed her eyes to dry them. "I didn't know that the rods could be used that way."

"Oh yes, they are very versatile. It is quite amazing what can be done with them. Anyway, I must be going now. That has quite tired me." Kirra stood up. "And it is so damn hot too. Now be warned Carla, there is a storm coming, the biggest storm for years. It will arrive suddenly and out of a clear sky too. Be sure that you don't get caught out in it."

"I will be on the lookout for it." Carla stood up and gave Kirra a friendly parting hug. "Thanks again Kirra for what you just did for me, I will give what you said a lot of thought."

Kirra walked back in the direction of the farm. As Carla looked at the straw bale Kirra had been sitting on, she thought that it now looked untidy and out of place. So she dragged it to the side and placed it neatly against the wall. Then Carla began to walk up to the fallen tree as she listened to the sound of Henry in the distance hammering the wooden fencing posts into the ground with his sledgehammer.

When she arrived at the fallen tree she was just about to open her tote bag when Ginger jumped up on the shelf, "Where did you come from little fellow?" She gave him a few biscuits and then made a fuss of him.

After a while, he jumped off the wooden shelf and lay on the grass under the tree, in a shady spot. Carla took several items out of her tote bag and placed them out on the wooden shelf. Then she lifted her feet onto the horizontal tree and lay back against the upright branch. At first, she lay there just chilling out and watching Henry working on his new fence. After some time, he walked back to the trailer and took a bottle out of a rucksack, and took a long drink from it.

She thought *He must be getting so hot doing that kind of work, especially today out in the open sun.*

Henry began to unbutton his shirt. Carla couldn't resist reaching for the binoculars to take a closer look. As he took off his shirt he unknowingly revealed, to the unseen Carla, his full strong muscular chest. As she looked on she whispered, "Oh my, oh my. Maybe I should try some of that after all." As she lowered the binoculars, she groaned and reluctantly said, "No Carla, I must not."

Her inner voice commented, *remember what Kirra said not all that long ago, "Oh, but you will, my dear, I can promise you*

102

that. Many have told me that once they found themselves in his arms, they just melted like butter. I have never seen a single female, staying at The Old Mill on holiday, deny herself that particular pleasure."

"I might have expected more support from you."

If you want more support from me, then you should listen to me more often.

"What are you on about. I listen to you."

You don't

"I do indeed."

You, do not, not, not!

"Go on then, give me an example of a time when I have not listened to you."

You fail to listen to me every time I say that you need to take up singing again.

"Well, that is a bit different."

No, it is not. The only thing that makes it any different in your mind is the knowledge of what your so-called new friend Lying Lynn thinks about your singing talents. She never should have written that hurtful article about you. Lynn isn't even qualified to judge you as a singer, in any way whatsoever. After reading that article you took it to heart, instead of remembering all of the many excellent comments and reviews from many other people you received in the past. You can sing, believe me. How many people have told you to drop Lying Lynn as a friend? Even Kirra said so today.

"You know I feel sorry for her, you know I do."

Carla for the millionth time, tell her to sling her hook and start singing again.

Carla lowered her head a little and rubbed her forehead with her hands. "I know, you are right. The time has now come to admit it to myself. For some reason, in the last few years, I have allowed others to walk all over me, when I really shouldn't have. Why did I let that happen to me?"

Tears began to form and a few ran down her cheeks, which she rubbed away with her hand.

"Oh, it's too hot for tears."

She drank some water from a bottle in her bag and tried to compose herself again.

Look at Henry working away. That will cheer you up.

"Right then," Carla stated affirmatively, "All this is going to stop. When my tears have dried up I am going to sing my first song in a long time. Then I am going to sing another one. After that, I am going to get my sketchbook out and draw whatever I fancy drawing, because drawing is another thing too many people say I should give up doing. I enjoy both singing and drawing and I will do them both if I want to, and if other people don't like it, then that is their problem. I will not compromise myself any longer. Finally, as for me and Lying Lynn," she sighed, "Somehow I am going to have to break off our friendship. That might be tricky."

You do not need to worry about that, because very soon that will all be sorted out for you.

"What, are you physic now too?"

Just then, a text came through from Lying Lynn, *I have been thinking hard all morning about why Sophie Archer has escaped me so far, and I keep arriving at the same conclusion, somehow it must have been you. I don't know how you did it, but I will never forgive you for this. You and I are through.*

Other People's Plans
Chapter 8

A couple of hours later Carla had indeed sung two songs and thoroughly enjoyed herself doing so. With newfound energy, she now had drawn two new drawings in her sketchbook. The first was a very detailed close up section of tree bark from a branch very close to where she was sitting. The second was a small robin, which Carla had to draw very quickly after it landed on a twig close to her. Although it may have been less detailed than her first drawing, she found the end result very satisfying.

Carla took a few moments to see how Henry was getting on with his new fence. He appeared to be digging a hole now, presumably for a gatepost.

Carla began to reflect on her singing career so far. Just before the hurtful article Lying Lynn had written about her singing talents, Carla had been receiving a growing number of bookings for her tribute act performances. For a moment, she was reminded of how she felt on stage, giving her best vocal tribute performance, reminiscent of so many great female artists.

"Maybe I should not have cast my net so wide in the past, and just specialised on only one act?"

No, that is not you. You have always been very interested in many artists and their work. Stick to the way you do things and give it your best, while being true to yourself.

Carla began to think about her next move to help her get back into tribute act singing.

"Maybe I could post a new video on *YouTube*. My channel has thousands of likes and subscribers, but I have not added any new content to it for a long time. I am sure my fans must be hungry for something new from me."

Why don't you pull your phone out and record a video with you singing some kind of solo, without any music accompaniment at all? Only the very best singers can carry that off. You are and always have been good enough to do that.

"That is an interesting idea. I remember listening to 'Tom's Diner' by Suzanne Vega, there were two versions of that song, one with musical backing and one without. The version without any musical accompaniment gained quite a lot of notoriety as result. Although that particular song does not feel like the right one for me, so what shall I sing? I would need a song, which is best sung slowly, I believe. Maybe something from *Fleetwood Mac*, such as *Dreams* or *Sara*? "

Two very good choices vocally and excellent tribute act material, but the lyrics of those songs leave gaps for instrumental sections, which you would be left struggling to fill.

"I suppose that is true."

Carla laughed at a passing thought. "Fleetwood Mac's Rhiannon has the perfect lyrics for this place, Rhiannon rings like a bell through the night and, wouldn't you love to love her?"

Stop it and get serious.

"Okay then. The song, *How Deep Is Your Love,* by the *Bee Gees,* that might work. And there are a lot of cover versions by male and female artists too."

It would indeed be a good choice, but would it showcase the best of your voice?

"*I Will Always Love You,* by *Whitney Houston,* now that is a real belter of a song, I would love to do that one, but maybe that is a bit too powerful for what I need here."

Carla laughed at her next thought, "*Killing Me Softly with His Song,* By *Roberta Flack."*

No way at all. While that song does have many excellent qualities, there is no escaping its sad heavy feel.

"*Amazing Grace* and *Ave Maria* are two excellent well known songs, which are perfect for an unaccompanied solo."

That is true, but as your inner guide and adviser, I must recommend a song you know very well, have always enjoyed singing, and a song that you have used so many times as a vocal warm-up.

"You keep saying that you are my guide and adviser; whatever? But I think that you are right about the choice of song though, it would be the perfect song for this because the slower you sing the lyrics, the better the vocals get. *The Windmills of Your Mind,* it is then."

Too many singers think all you have to do is sing each line of a song, but as you know only too well, and have demonstrated so many times before, the best singers sing not just every line perfectly, but every word perfectly.

"Okay then, it is time for me to record a new song for my video channel. Later on, when I return to *The Old Mill* I will watch the video through again and then upload it to YouTube."

Carla then took out her phone and pressed the video record button, "Hi everyone, I know it has been a while, too long in fact, but I can promise you that I am back now and I am here to stay. I am sitting out in the open countryside on the hottest day of the year so far, and I have decided, quite spontaneously to sing something very special for you now, without any musical accompaniment."

She began by stretching out the first word of the song 'round' out to its fullest with a smoky smouldering vocal tone and then continued to bring every detailed vocal nuance out of every word of the song. Vocally visiting so many great highs and lows of emotions, drama and suspense, combined with an underlying poetic melancholy as the song unfolded.

As she sang it, she knew that she was delivering her best rendition of this great song and even felt a tingle go right through her on a number of occasions, at several key points in the song. The concluding line of the song reached its climax when the final word of the song was executed to near perfection, as Carla's eyes came to a close.

After a few seconds, she slowly began to open them again as a gentle smile formed, content in the knowledge that she had just given her best ever performance of that song. Then she pressed the video stop-record button on her phone, and much to her surprise she heard someone begin clapping enthusiastically. Carla turned towards the applause and smiled with appreciation as the man came into view. He was an older gentleman. She noticed he was wearing a safari shirt and shorts and he was carrying a very large black umbrella.

"I hope you didn't mind me hiding back here. After walking over the brow of the hill, I heard you singing, and because I did not want to put you off, I kept close to the hedge and out of sight as I approached. I must say you are a truly excellent singer."

"Thank you, I am pleased that you enjoyed listening to it."

"Oh yes, I did indeed. If you don't mind Miss I will walk around to your side of the tree. It will be easier to talk with you then."

Carla waited as the man walked around to her side, as he approached Carla swung her legs off the horizontal tree and placed her feet back on the ground.

"Would you mind Miss if I sit on that tree with you for a few moments? It is a very hot day for an old boy like me, you know."

He sat down beside her and wiped his brow, as he said, "Have you seen that damn fool over there. He is banging in wooden stakes with a sledgehammer on the hottest day of the year. You know the old saying, *only mad dogs and Englishmen go out in the midday sun.*"

Carla chuckled, "Yes, he does seem to be determined to do it today of all days. I am not sure why that is either."

"Oh, it is indeed a strange pastime on a hot day like this Carla my girl."

Carla looked at the old man curiously, "How did you know my name was Carla? I suppose you met Kirra or one of the other girls from the stables and they told you my name?"

"Oh no, no one told me your name. It was just a lucky guess that is all. You look like a Carla to me," he said dismissively, as he smiled and gave Carla a playful wink, and then he added, "Of course that man over there could be putting on some kind of macho display for your benefit, in order to wow a fair maiden. You know what some guys are like."

Carla looked in Henry's direction, "Surely not, it is an intriguing idea though, but I can't believe in that one."

The man laughed. "Actually, when I walked this way last week he was working over there on the same short section of fence, while another lady was sitting where you are now."

"Now I know that you must be joking." She laughed.

"Am I?" He said as he wiped his brow again. "I loved the way you sang that lovely old song. You sang with such feeling, it was a real pleasure for me listening to you. I assume that you must be a professional singer?"

"I was what you might describe as semi-professional, because it was not my full-time job, but I was getting busier over time. I have taken a break from it in recent times. I am beginning to regret that now; because, if I am honest with myself, I was an up and coming singer in my chosen area of the profession. Everything was beginning to come together for me, so I never should have stopped singing."

"You mention your area of the singing profession, what might that be?"

"I am a tribute act singer. Some tribute act singers specialise in just one artist or band, but a few like me sing a tribute to a number of the greatest female artists."

"That sounds very interesting. No wonder you can sing so well. I have seen some tribute acts myself over the years, the best of them are extremely good and make for a good night out."

"So that was me, singing in pubs and clubs, to begin with, and then I progressed to larger venues, like theatres and events. My video channel on YouTube was very successful too."

"Why did you stop?"

Carla shook her head. "I let one bad review from a journalist bring me down. Stopping singing felt like the right thing to do at the time, but I regret it now, I really do. To be honest with you, it was only earlier today that I turned my thoughts around about the whole thing. That is why I was singing that song while recording it for my video channel."

Carla sighed. "I must also confess something quite bizarre. After that journalist wrote the article that stopped my singing career, I somehow allowed her into my life and to become a friend. I never should have done that or allowed her any closer to me. That was a huge mistake. Looking back, I can't believe that I ever let that happen, but I actually felt sorry for her. She has her own pains and troubles in life, many in fact, yet she brings a wide assortment of hurt and pain to others without a care."

"She doesn't sound like a very nice person, but you must be a special kind of soul if you wanted to show kindness and friendship towards her after she wrote that article about you. Be pleased that you have rare qualities, they set you apart from the crowd."

"It has been a day of changes for me. I appear to have reached a turning point in my life. I have made some positive decisions and found my direction in life again."

"I very much approve of turning points, making some positive decisions and finding your direction in life. I am very pleased for you Carla, my girl."

Carla laughed a little. "Look at us two strangers talking so freely, as if we have known each other for years. That has happened to me twice today, earlier I was talking to a lady called Kirra for the first time and that conversation turned out to be quite thought-provoking."

"Since we are chatting so freely please tell me a bit more about Carla, what else apart from singing interests you."

"Right from childhood, I have always been quite good at drawing. It has remained a hobby of mine and when I have some free time I still find it a very enjoyable and relaxing thing to do."

Carla reached behind her and picked up her sketchbook from the wooden shelf.

"I must say this old fallen tree is very well set up. I have never seen a tree with a shelf before. Very ingenious."

Carla then showed the man some of her drawings, "That drawing of the little robin was the hardest to draw, because I had to draw as much of him as I could very quickly before he flew away, and then draw the rest from memory."

"I have never been very good at drawing myself, but even so I can appreciate your skills from what you have shown me."

Carla put the sketchbook back on the shelf and then the man added, "I can see two books on that wooden shelf too."

"Yes, I am staying here at *The Old Mill* on holiday and those books are from there, the binoculars too. I have been trying a bit of bird watching, but I don't think that is really my thing. However, the binoculars have come in handy, a time or two." She laughed.

"I hope you are not suggesting that binoculars come in handy for being a bit nosy from the high ground offered by this tree," he joked.

"I don't know what you could possibly mean?" she replied with a faint laugh.

"I know the other book on your shelf very well indeed, *Think and Grow Rich*. When I was younger, I read that book a lot and it helped me enormously, I still read it occasionally even now. Over the years, I have met so many people who have read that book regularly and try to absorb its content and make it a key part of how they live their life. Every time I meet such a person, I find that I have a successful person stood in front of me, or a person whose ship is just about to come in."

"Some people have been telling me similar things about that book in the past and recently. I have only just picked it up myself this week, but I have read it cover to cover now. I will get my own copy when I get home and continue to read it."

"That is an excellent idea. Incidentally, the word *Rich* in the book's title implies financial reward, but as you must know from reading it the book is not just about financial reward, it covers every aspect of success and making your dreams and goals come true."

"Yes, I can see that. The book applies as much to me as a singer wanting to grow in my profession, as it would for anyone wanting to grow in theirs. *Think and Grow Rich,* could have been just as accurately titled, *Think and Grow Successful."*

"I can agree with you there," he said with a warm smile. Then he slowly stood up. "I feel better for my short rest, and I have very much enjoyed talking with you. Although I would truly love to stay longer, I must leave before the storm comes; that is why I'm carrying this large umbrella, in case I get caught out in it."

"Oh come now, there is not going to be any storm today surely. I checked the weather forecast this morning and it is going to be just another long hot day today. Maybe even a new high temperature wise."

He gave a knowing smile and then said, "Carla my girl, like I said it has been a pleasure talking with you. My name is Ted by the way, just so you know, in readiness for the next time we meet. But in case we don't meet again, please let me share some

113

wisdom with you based on our conversation and in the spirit of that book, *Think and Grow Rich.*"

He looked pleased that Carla was listening to him with interest.

"Anyone can have a dream in life, and many may even set a goal to achieve it. There is no greater life skill than goal-attraction, and yet it is something that almost no one understands. While many think they do, in truth only a rare few can truly claim in all honesty that they do understand goal-attraction. As a result, far too few people achieve their dreams and goals in life. That is why great books such as, *Think and Grow Rich,* are so very important to anyone serious about achieving their dreams and goals in life. Dreams and goals in life are vitally important to an individual. When correctly used and applied over time, they develop in a person a rare collection of personal qualities: direction, clarity of mind, life purpose and ultimately a form of happiness and contentment that many will never experience. Without those qualities, that only an applied understanding of goal attraction can ultimately deliver, then a person is vulnerable to the influences from the dreams and goals of stronger minds, more committed minds. Ultimately, you have two choices in life, you can peruse your own dreams and goals in life with a real committed burning desire and expect to ultimately achieve them over time, or else you will spend your own life helping others to achieve their dreams and goals. Other people's dreams and goals will come dressed up within their well-laid plans, totally unnoticed by the crowd. Other people's dreams and goal rarely involve great plans for you, no matter how much you may help them to achieve theirs."

Ted paused and gave Carla a friendly smile, "I wish you well Carla, in everything you do."

He then glanced in Henry's direction, with a look of mistrust and spoke one last time before leaving, "Too many people become consumed by, and react to, the events in the environment immediately around them, and that all too human folly comes at the very high price of not attracting their dreams and goals in life. Don't slip into other people's worlds Carla no matter how tempting and attractive they may first appear."

The Many Lovers of Henry Farmer
Chapter 9

After Ted had walked away, Carla sat on the tree thinking for some time. Her two conversations that day with Ted and Kirra had both been very thought-provoking and insightful. Now she understood herself better, and could see where she had gone wrong and lost her direction in life in recent times.

Content in the knowledge of what she now needed to do to get things back on track when this holiday is over, she said to herself, "This holiday has worked out just fine so far. It really has. I have had the chance to think things through and talk with people who have been very helpful in bringing new clarity to my thoughts."

Carla waited to see if her inner voice had something to say. Nothing came for some time and then, *I have to say that I agree with you. After this holiday we can go home and make exciting new things happen. Hopefully, I can now take a back seat again for a while. You know what you need to do and which direction you must go in; so you don't need me just at the moment, but I will be here if you do.*

"It seems only polite to say thank you to you. We will talk again some more my inner friend, when we get home. I think all I need to do now is chill out and relax for the rest of my holiday so that I am in top form when I get home."

Carla let her mind go blank for a few minutes as she stared at nothing in particular. As she returned to normality she

116

became aware of the relative silence of the day. Due to the heat and stillness of the day the only sound to be heard was Henry as he hammered wooden posts into the ground.

She felt like drawing something trivial and light-hearted, so she took off her sunhat and sunglasses and placed them on the horizontal trunk of the tree. Then she dressed the sunhat to look like a face by using her sunglasses for eyes, and a few twigs for a nose and mouth.

"Perfect," she said proudly as she began to draw the scene. When she was about halfway through drawing it something drew her attention back to the farm. She saw someone standing near the gate to the farm lane as if they intended to enter the field. Not recognising who it was Carla picked up her binoculars to take a closer look.

"Oh my, oh my. Is that really you Marie? What a transformation."

Carla remembered Fiona's words from the night of the barbeque, *"Marie is a girl who moves through cycles. Most of the time she acutely feels the loss of her man and looks very unhappy, then slowly over a period of a few weeks she gradually brightens up and lets her hair down. When she feels like her old self again, she makes a play for Henry and parties with him like some wild untamed animal. Honestly, Marie is the wildest girl here, no doubt about it; when she really gets going, she makes the rest of us like nuns."*

As Carla looked on through the binoculars she studied Marie's transformation. Gone was the long blue summer dress and the unkempt ponytail. Also, there was no missing the absence of her face full of pain, as Marie stood there looking bold and confident, wearing denim shorts and a button blouse.

As Marie looked towards the field, she appeared to be searching for Henry. When she found him, a sultry look came across her face.

"I never thought I would see that kind of expression on Marie's hurt face," Carla commented. Then she was even more surprised to see Marie begin to unbutton her shirt.

"Oh my, it looks as if Marie forgot to put her bra on when she dressed this morning."

Marie began to tie the bottom two sides of her shirt into a knot, while being careful to leave a long wide open V neck.

"My, oh my, Marie," Carla said in amazement, and then she remembered what Tracy had also said about Marie at the barbeque, *"I've seen it happen many times before with Marie. Actually, I think at the moment she is gradually improving day by day. So some truly wild times are not far away. It is quite a transformation to behold, believe me, she becomes so free and loses all of her inhibitions."*

"Quite a transformation indeed, but then nothing would surprise me around here anymore."

Carla shook her head a little and returned to her drawing. As she added some fine shading with her pencil, it began to unexpectedly smudge.

"Now what is that all about?" She asked herself as she drew the sketchbook closer to inspect it, only to find to her surprise that the paper now had a small damp patch on it. "I wonder where that came from." Looking around her, she could not understand why her sketchbook now had a damp patch on it. Then she heard a splash sound as a large droplet of water landed on the top of the sketchbook. In disbelief, Carla turned the book over and shook the water droplet off.

Carla then looked around and above her again, "I don't get it, where can that water be coming from; there is nothing but a clear blue open sky, not a cloud in sight."

She questioned in disbelief. After putting the sketchbook on the shelf, she got down from the tree trunk to take a look at things from another viewpoint. As she stood there looking at the tree she heard more water droplets landing around her. Within a few seconds, there were several water droplets on the tree trunk. Carla looked at the sky again, "Well it can't be rain. There isn't a cloud in the sky."

Then Carla remembered what Kirra had said to her earlier that morning, *"Now be warned Carla, there is a storm coming, the biggest storm for years. It will arrive suddenly and out of a clear sky too. Be sure that you don't get caught in it."*

Carla shrugged and looked around her again in disbelief. "Surely not a storm out of a clear blue sky, no way. Such things cannot happen. No wonder all the other girls were laughing at you Kirra for saying such a draft thing."

More and more heavy drops of water fell.

"I hate to admit it, but clear blue sky or not, that looks like rain to me."

A strong breeze past by her and left Carla feeling ill at ease as she watched the pages in her sketchbook be blown over as it lay on the shelf. From somewhere unseen, Carla heard the rumble of thunder. She glanced over in Henry's direction to see him stood looking at the sky. Then, almost in an instant, heavy rain began to fall, as she looked at the dry wood across the tree trunk she saw it turn to soaking wet almost in an instant.

Carla moved in closer to the fallen tree as she tried to find some shelter from the rain amongst its branches. In a very short

119

space of time, the rain grew heavier and heavier still, as the thickness of rain coming down reduced the sunlight getting through and transformed everything in appearance into a unified greyness.

Carla looked back to the farm, but with the ever reducing field of vision caused by the storm, it was already very difficult to see that far away, so she felt that it was no longer an option to run back to *The Old Mill*.

She turned her attention to the old waney-edge wooden barn, where she could just about make out its outline in the distance as thunder and lightning now crashed and flashed ever more violently about her.

Carla was struggling to take in the enormous, almost instant change in weather as the storm appeared to intensify even more. She was now already soaking wet through and realised that staying by the tree was no longer a good idea.

Leaving everything she had brought with her behind Carla began to run as fast as she could towards the old barn. As she ran the ever-increasing storm lashed so much water in her face that she was struggling to see and find her way to the old barn. Her feet slashed and dragged their way through torrents of water, which the sloping field had created, and in many places the water was already higher than her ankles. The relatively short journey from the fallen tree to the shelter offered by the old wooden barn now felt to Carla like a marathon of endurance as it continued. When she finally reached the open doors of the old wooden barn, she felt a huge relief as she came running through them at full pelt. Carla had built up so much momentum running through the storm that she now struggled to slow down and landed heavily on the small square bales at the back of the barn. She stayed there for some time panting heavily as her heart raced from the strong exertion of the run through the storm.

After allowing time for her breathing and heartbeat to return to normal, she turned around and walked forward a little. As she looked at the scene outside through the barn's open doors, she saw the rain coming down as hard as ever and the outside world looked almost black now due to the blocked out sunlight.

She lowered her head to look at herself. She was now standing in a pool of water, as her saturated clothes dripped. Her clothes clung tightly to her, and as she ran both hands down the front of her shirt she forced water free from them, which added to the pool of water under her feet. She began to take off her shirt, which resisted being removed as it clung to her tightly. When it finally came off Carla began to wring it out with her hands and was amazed by how much water came out of it.

In an odd combination of anger and frustration, she groaned as she then threw the wet shirt defiantly in the general direction of the door, where it landed only a few feet away from the rain outside. Still feeling quite annoyed with being wet through, she then squeezed both of her bra cups to see how wet they were, but due to the light material they were made from only a small amount of water came out of them. Next, she slapped the front of her jeans, which gave off a squelching sound as the water came out of them.

Carla let out a frustrated sigh, and was just about to unbutton her jeans to wring them out, when she was momentarily distracted by a bright flash of lightning outside against the relative darkness of the barn. She stood waiting for the sound of thunder, which would surely follow, and when it crashed it was so loud that Carla jumped.

Immediately after that, Henry came running in from the storm at full pelt, he too was running with such momentum that he ran into the straw bales at the back of the barn before he could stop. He turned around panting and trying to catch his breath. Although he was not wearing a shirt, he too was soaked through. They silently looked at each other dripping in water. Carla looked as drops of water ran off his head and then down his strong well-toned muscular chest. They both exchanged an awkward smile.

"Where's your shirt, Carla?" Henry enquired struggling for breath.

"I was just taking my clothes off to wring the water out of them, but I am not sure if it is even worth the effort of doing that."

"Maybe, maybe not? Perhaps it is best just to wait out the storm and then go back to the farm and dry off properly before changing into something dry."

Lightning flashed and then there was an unbelievably loud crash of thunder overhead, which caused them both to cower down upon hearing it.

"It can't get any louder than that one, can it?" Carla said nervously as she moved a little closer to Henry for comfort. Then another flash of lightning came, immediately followed by a crash of thunder so many times louder than the first, and so loud and violent that they both jumped, scared into each other arms.

Carla was now shaking as Henry tried to comfort her in his arms cradling her head in his wet chest, which was still beating strongly after his run to the barn. The storm then appeared to abate a little, but they both remained together.

In his arms, Carla could smell faint traces of his Spanish aftershave and found it quite intoxicating. She indulged herself in the experience of being in his strong muscular arms with her face pressed against his chest. She felt herself weakening and wanting to yield to him.

Then without a thought she reached up and kissed him on the cheek, "Oh Henry," she said in a quiet, loving tone of voice, before returning her head onto his chest.

Henry then began to caress her back and shoulders, and she couldn't hide how much she revelled in every moment of it as the sense of want and expectation grew inside her. She lifted her head again to look at him which led naturally into a passionate kiss.

As they parted from the kiss Henry asked, "Do you want this?"

She nodded in the affirmative. Henry took Carla by the hand and led her to a loose heap of straw lying in front of the stacked bales. Carla gazed at the makeshift bed in the anticipation of things to come. They fell together onto the straw facing each other, with no more words needing to be spoken. Their eyes met, and then they slowly moved in closer. Just as they were about to begin a long, lingering kiss they were interrupted by the loud sound of a dog barking. They both looked towards the barn entrance to see Max sitting there soaking wet.

Henry commented, "Well that's a rare sight indeed. I can't remember the last time I saw him move off that front porch, and I have certainly never seen him in this barn before."

Carla sat up a little, as quite unexpectedly her inner voice said, *Maybe it's a sign?* Max shook himself vigorously, in a vain attempt to dry off, before barking once more and running back out into the storm.

Henry sat up and softly said, "Now Carla, where were we?" Carla remained silent for a few moments, lost in thought, as she recalled many elements of her conversations that day with Kirra and Ted. Much to Henry's surprise, she stood up and walked forward a few paces.

Henry stood up also and enquired, "Is everything alright Carla?"

Carla then slowly turned around to face Henry, "No!" she said firmly. "No this is not happening." She momentarily paused again and then looked Henry in the eye. "I suspect that we were just lying together on the straw in the same place that you and that young model lay together?"

Henry looked a little surprised by the question, but replied reassuringly in a soft comforting tone of voice, "Well yes Carla, I will not lie to you, we did. But she is now long gone, this moment is ours, and this special time belongs to us and us alone."

Carla looked into his eyes and firmly spoke, "Not any longer. That moment has just passed us by forever, I can promise you."

Henry spoke calmly, "Come now, Carla. If something is wrong, please tell me what it is. The last thing I would ever want to do is hurt your feelings in some way. Please give me the chance to put this right."

"You can't put this right Henry because I can now see right through you. I suspect that you have always had a certain gift with the ladies and never had any trouble attracting them. I also suspect that you learnt how to be successful in business a long time ago, and later on, you took those same business success principles and combined them with your natural gifts with us ladies and created *Prosperity Farm and Stables* as your playground. The result is that you have now given me an entirely new understanding of the term, millionaire-playboy. So, please tell me Henry, am I right, is that more or less what you have done here?"

Henry sighed a little. "Well, I would not have put it quite like that, but for the most part, you are right. You wouldn't believe how much study and research it took to build up that kind of specialist knowledge to carry off such a thing. But, we have the opportunity to be together now. I can promise you that it will be a special loving moment in time that you will treasure forever. Please don't let this moment pass us by. You may well later regret missing it if you do."

"Yes, I suspect I will always wonder about letting this moment pass me by, but pass me by it will; even though it is so very tempting to stay here with you. My time here these past few days has been time well spent. When I arrived here I was a person who had lost my way in life, and now I have rediscovered it again. I realise now that I never actually lost my way at all, instead, I let others hold me back and drag me down. My future is in my hands. I will stand up for myself. I will not let other people drag me down any longer, and I will not be drawn into other people's plans or their false worlds, and I certainly will not become a plaything in another person's game of love heart dice. I know who I am. I know what I want in life and how to achieve it."

Carla took a deep breath and said, "So, storm or no storm, I must remove myself from the great temptation that you truly are. So, I will walk over to the barn doorway, then I will collect my soaking wet shirt, and calmly walk out of here, back to *The Old Mill*. After all, I am already soaked through anyway, so what will a bit more matter?"

Henry thought for a moment and was just about to reply when something else caught his attention. Carla could see from Henry's expression that there must be someone else now standing in the doorway, someone that Henry knew well.

Carla turned around to see Marie standing in the doorway, soaking wet from the storm, but looking red-hot and seductive. As Carla watched Marie walk over to them. Never before had Carla seen Marie walk like that, she oozed sexiness with every exaggerated swing in every step.

Just before she reached them Marie said, "I see that you have taken your top off Carla, but at least you didn't start without me."

She pulled Henry towards her, kissed him and then sank into his arms. Marie then looked very happy and content as she drew so much comfort from being in Henry's arms.

Carla said coldly, "It's alright Marie, I was just leaving, anyway."

Marie replied seductively, "Don't be like that Carla, stop here and join in the fun. You don't know what you're missing. Outside Mother Nature is unleashing a very powerful force. Stay here with us, and we three can unleash an incredible wild power of nature all of our own. Don't leave when the party is just about to begin and miss experiencing something that you will never regret and never forget."

Henry held out an arm as if to invite her into their shared embrace.

"I would love to join you, I really would, but I am not going to give away the best of me to you both so lightly."

Carla then walked over to the doorway and picked her wet shirt from the floor. She looked outside, while the storm had lessened a bit. She still did not want to venture into it, but she knew that she must, for her own sake.

Just then Marie called out to her from Henry's embrace, "Carla, come on now, you don't want to go out there again. Come over here and join us. You know you want to."

Carla looked towards them and replied, "As I see it, I have two choices, I can leave here right now and maybe I will one day regret that, or I can stay here in the dry, but if I do that, there is the very real chance that I will wave goodbye to my own dreams and goals and become, just another one of the many lovers of Henry Farmer."

And with that, she turned around and walked out into the storm.

I

After reading this book, please sign and date it, and then share this book with another person.

The Well-Travelled Book Series

To purchase other titles from The Well-Travelled Book Series or to post a book review, please go to –

www.tonybrassington.com

or

www.amazon.co.uk

There is also a Facebook page for *The Well-Travelled Book Series*

Where Has This Book Travelled?

Please fill in your name below and then share this book with someone else.

Maybe take a photograph of this book in whatever part of the world you have read it in, and then post it on social media.

Names of people who have read this book	Date	Where this book has been read and travelled to

Printed in Great Britain
by Amazon